Mrs Dunc
26 Sea
Bexhill-on-Sea.

THE MARRIAGE OF CLAUDIA

THE MARRIAGE OF CLAUDIA

To
WILLIAM BROWN MELONEY

THE MARRIAGE OF CLAUDIA

By

ROSE FRANKEN

THE BOOK CLUB
121 CHARING CROSS ROAD,
LONDON, W.C.2

MADE AND PRINTED IN GREAT BRITAIN BY
MORRISON AND GIBB LTD., LONDON AND EDINBURGH

ONE

SHE WAS GLAD that the children had not come along, although they begged to, and David said that the experience would not hurt them. " I want to see you sell the farm," Matthew clamoured, as if selling a farm were a seasonal thing like filling a silo. Bobby, however, showed a deep and private grief. " I have to say good-bye to the cows," he said.

He seemed older and younger than his nine years. Claudia was careful not to kiss him. " I'll say good-bye to the cows for you," she promised.

" Why didn't you want them to come ? " David asked her, as they drove beyond the city limits.

" They'd be in the way, there's so much to do at the last minute."

" Nonsense," he said largely, " there's nothing left to do but sign the transfer of the deed."

She didn't bother to argue with him. Signing papers was the least of it. He didn't seem to realize what it meant to give up the only home they had ever known—except the two-room apartment on the East River the first year they were married. It was funny that the furniture they had bought for the little flat were the only things they were keeping to put in storage—the Adam commode, the Queen Anne gaming table, the old wing chairs, and the desk. These had been the nucleus of their lives, and the rest had been added to meet the needs of living—beds and mattresses and cribs and carpets. " It's nice that we needn't be ashamed of what we started with," Claudia said. " Most people disown their first mistakes."

" That's because you married an architect," David pointed out smugly. " I didn't let you go in for a lot of second-rate reproductions."

" Now wait a minute, one thing I always had was good taste," Claudia stuck up for herself. The minute she said it her blood ran cold. Suppose he were to retort that she had shown her good taste when she chose him as a husband ? He didn't, of course. He simply took a great jump into the middle of their hearts, and put his arm around her and said softly, " Don't let selling the place get you down, darling."

" I won't." She smiled faintly. " Experience and all that."

Thank you for the experience. It was more than she'd bargained for, and more than David had bargained for too, although he wouldn't admit it. This last drive up from New York was like a trip to the cemetery, with the end of it letting go of something that had become a very part of their existence. The farm had held them secure through birth and death and war; it had contributed to their happiness and accommodated their grief. This was not the moment to remember frozen water pipes and leaking roofs, to say nothing of feed and labour bills and countless veterinary visits for an ailing cow or pig. No. Already the thorns were blanketed in memory. The farm was assuming the sanctity of death.

It had never looked lovelier than to-day. The meadows ran out into the autumn sun as if they would burst their fences, but the little salt-box house sat demurely in the bend of the road, as it had sat for a century and a half, and would, if Nancy Riddle could keep her hands off its façade, continue to sit for years to come. "You really are a good architect," Claudia granted, "the way you made all the changes and additions in the rear. To look at the house from the front, you'd think butter wouldn't melt in its mouth."

David slowed to a stop, and they might have been seeing the place for the first time. "I'll never forget," Claudia mused, "how disappointed I was. You told me it was a magnificent entrance, and I expected no less than an impressive mansion set back in an arch of trees."

"Old houses never sat back from the road," David informed her, as if she hadn't learned that by this time. "However, it is a magnificent door. This house is as pure an example of early architecture as exists in New England."

"I know it, only it took me a little time to appreciate it," said Claudia humbly. "Do you think Nancy Riddle appreciates it?"

"No," said David.

"Doesn't it rankle a little that she's only buying it for the help to live in?"

"No," said David again.

She regarded him curiously. "You still feel that the farm has served its purpose, and it's right for us to give it up?"

"Yes," he said.

Claudia sighed. "I agree with you, but simply out of habit. I mean, I don't exactly have the same conviction that it's served its purpose—although I'm willing to believe," she added hastily, as she saw indecision cloud his eyes. " I mean to say," she made clear, " that I'm not regretting it a bit."

" That's good," he said. He put his hand over hers for an instant before he took the wheel again. " You never were a whiner," he mentioned briefly.

Edward didn't hear the car turn in the drive. They found him separating milk like mad in the little dairy off the barn.

" It's too bad we won't have enough cream to take back to New York," David began a little too jovially.

" The milk piled up on me," Edward explained. " I haven't taken any to market for the last two days."

Claudia said, " Wouldn't you think those silly cows would have enough sense to stop ? We'll never use all that." She peered into a foaming pail. " Skimmed milk always fools me ; it looks so rich and bubbly."

" Just a lot of bluff," said David, to make conversation.

Edward took him literally. " It is good for the pigs and chickens, they will have a fine farewell supper. The storage people called for everything early this morning," he went on. " There's not much left to do. The auctioneers are inside now. They said if the weather held up good tomorrow, they could hold the sale on the lawn, cattle and everything. Nobody thought we'd get a warm spell this close to Thanksgiving." He paused to rub his elbow over his face, and Claudia noticed that he'd had a fresh haircut, which might have been the reason he looked peaked.

" It's damned unseasonable," said David, who suddenly looked peaked too. " Where's Bluster ? "

" Locked up in the kennel," said Edward. " He's been nervous all day. I always knew little dogs felt things in the air, but this is the first time I ever saw a Great Dane have that kind of sense."

" I don't know why people think Great Danes are stupid," Claudia protested.

" They're not bright," said David. " I don't see Shakespeare around either."

" I put him in my room and closed the door," said Edward. " He'd be off hiding if I didn't. He won't want to leave here. Cats favour places more than people."

" Not Shakespeare," said Claudia. " We've had him over ten years. He'd die without us."

" I expect he'll miss the farm more," said Edward.

"We'll make it up to him. I bought a make-believe tree for him to scratch on."

"You hope," David amended. "Let's go in the house. I left my canes in the attic."

The auctioneer had already appropriated the canes. Tied up into two knobby bundles, they stood sentry on either side of an array of china and vases. "Hey," said David indignantly, "those are mine."

The auctioneer was apologetic, but firm. "Sorry, sir," he said. "Mrs. Riddle said that everything that was left in the house after the storage people went was to be sold."

"Not these," said David with equal firmness and stuck them under his arm and carried them to the car.

Claudia stood watching him. She saw little white circles come around his nostrils, and she knew that it wasn't so much the canes—although he was a fool for canes—as the shock of seeing the house pulled to pieces and stacked up in piles ready to be auctioned off to the highest bidder. She concluded, with a degree of satisfaction, that he was not as detached as he thought he was. He doubtless felt, as she did, that it would have been less of a wrench to have just walked out and left everything the way it was—which had been Nancy Riddle's idea in the first place.

"I'll take the property lock, stock, and barrel," she had specified, "provided I can have immediate possession. Keep your favourite pieces, but leave all the rest of the stuff."

At that point, a scant few weeks ago, Nancy was buying the house for her farm superintendent who had six children and no furniture. At the last minute, however, he decided to leave, so she replaced him with a young couple who had no children and a great deal of furniture.

"Oh dear," said Claudia when she heard about it.

Nancy was every inch the gentleman in her bulging riding breeches. "This is my headache, not yours," she assured them brusquely. "I have no intention of going back on my original deal."

Naturally they took for granted that she was going to make arrangements for the young couple to store their furniture; they had no idea of what was in her mind until Edward telephoned them about the auction sale several days later. "The stock's going to be sold too," he said with a hint of heartbreak in his stoical Vermont voice. "Seems as if this new young feller don't care much about milking, seems as if a few Angus is all he guarantees to handle."

THE MARRIAGE OF CLAUDIA

" Then she should find another man," Claudia expostulated. " She's got a big nerve. It's bad enough she's selling the furniture, but she has no right to sell the cattle."

" She has every right," said David, who had little medical and legal trends running through him. " She can burn the property down to the ground if she wants to."

" I'd almost rather she would," Claudia said, and David had told her to stop wallowing in sentiment.

" He's doing quite a little wallowing himself," she thought, as she watched him charge out to the car with his bundles of canes. When he came back, though, he was overflowing with detachment again. " You're not human," she accused him.

He pushed a chair toward her. " Sit down until Nancy comes."

" I have to go upstairs."

" Go down here."

" I left a lot of hangers in my closet."

" Be strong-minded. Let them stay there."

" They were good ones. Pants hangers, too."

He was short of pants hangers. He let her go, but the hangers had disappeared. Nothing but a few distorted wire ones dangled from a hook. Everything else from the bedroom was gone too, except the beds. In a little while the doctor's wife came in, and Claudia knew why they had been left standing.

" Dear little Mrs. Naughton, how nice to see you ! " Mrs. Barry exclaimed, with her voice waving up and down along her prominent teeth. " This is really a great shock, your selling this lovely, lovely place ! "

" It's a shock to us, too," said Claudia, " but all in all it seemed the wise thing to do."

Mrs. Barry's elderly hand, with its old-fashioned gold wedding band, stroked the rail of a walnut footboard. " But where on earth will you live in New York ? It's so difficult to find a nice place these days—any sort of place—as far as I can gather."

" Fortunately," said Claudia, " we're staying on in Mrs. Van Doren's apartments."

" I only hope it won't be rented right out from under you, the way I hear most of them are," Mrs. Barry suggested, in sepulchral anticipation.

" It can't," said Claudia. " Mrs. Van Doren owned it. Now, of course, it belongs to Candy."

" Oh," said Mrs. Barry, somewhat disappointed. She sat

down on the edge of one of the beds and furtively tested the mattress under cover of conversation. " I understand Candy's been living with you since her mother died."

" Yes. She's been with us ever since Mrs. Van Doren went to England. That's why Elizabeth wanted us to take the apartment, so that Candy could come home from college on vacations."

" It almost seems," said Mrs. Barry with a little shiver, " as if Mrs. Van Doren knew she was going to die—the way she made preparations, I mean. Though Doctor told me, definitely, that it was quite unexpected. Just one of those things." Mrs. Barry shivered again. " We never know. Here one minute and gone the next."

Claudia shivered too. " Anyway, it was a dreadful blow to Candy," she reverted hastily.

Mrs. Barry nodded her head violently. " That's exactly what I told Doctor. Candy's lucky, I told him, to have you and your husband to turn to at such a time. A girl misses her mother at that age. I used to say, when they were up here in the summer, that they were more like sisters, they were so close. You and your mother were very much the same way, as I recall."

" Yes," said Claudia.

" Still, you were a married woman and it was easier for you."

" It's always hard," said Claudia, " no matter when you lose your mother."

" I suppose it is," said Mrs. Barry, " but it's harder to lose a child." She sighed deeply. " I lost two."

" Oh, how dreadful," Claudia breathed. She thought, unhappily, how little one knew of one's neighbours, and what a beast she was not to have liked Mrs. Barry more. " I didn't know—I'm so terribly sorry—how old were they ? " she asked in compassion.

" It was before they were born," said Mrs. Barry.

" Oh," said Claudia, almost as letdown as Mrs. Barry had been over the apartment.

" I often think," Mrs. Barry continued, using up the rest of her sigh, " that I was too young."

Too young for what, Claudia wondered.

" You see, I was only eighteen when I married Doctor," Mrs. Barry explained with a delicate clearing of her throat.

" So was I," said Claudia. (Not when I married Doctor, though.)

" You know, these really are lovely, lovely mattresses," Mrs. Barry burst out, as if she couldn't keep it to herself a moment longer. " They're almost as good as new."

The one that Mrs. Barry happened to be sitting on was practically new. David had often said that they should have taken turns with the beds, but they never got around to it, and besides, it was pleasanter to use the one next to the window.

" I'm thinking," Mrs. Barry confided—as if Claudia hadn't already guessed it—" of buying these beds, if they don't go too high. Doctor and I have always had a big four-poster, but I don't sleep so well any more, and Doctor does quite a bit of smoking before he goes to sleep. . . ." Mrs. Barry laughed lightly. " You know how it is—men, men, men. Was there never a bureau to these beds ? "

" No," said Claudia. " David designed the clothes closets large enough to hold built-in drawers and cupboards."

" Well, Doctor has his old walnut highboy anyway and it'll go very nicely," Mrs. Barry decided. She glanced at her watch. " He's late. He promised to meet me here."

" I just heard a car come in," said Claudia. " It might be Mrs. Riddle, though."

It was the Doctor. It was odd to see him walking in to look at beds with nobody in them. He took Claudia's hand in both of his and said, " Well, my dear, so you and your husband are deserting us. Shame on you."

" Yes, isn't it," Mrs. Barry interrupted. Her voice pulled at his coat-tails, as she plumped the side of the nearest mattress. " There they are, dear," she said tremulously. " Just as good as new. And soft. Feel how soft."

" Myself, I like a hard mattress," said Dr. Barry. " However, if you like them, my dear, you're the boss."

This time it was her eyes that clutched at him in mute entreaty. " But you're not even looking at them, dear ! You've got to be pleased too, you know."

Dr. Barry gave exactly the right answer. " The old four-poster was good enough for me, Charlotte," he said, " but go ahead if you want to be newfangled."

" Oh you," Charlotte pouted, and for a fleeting instant Claudia caught her looking as she must have looked when Doctor married her. She got red and quivery, but she kept her eye on the ball anyway. " Georgie darling, I want you to see a perfectly darling little old antique table downstairs too. With duck feet. You love duck feet, dear."

Claudia debated whether or not to disillusion Mrs. Barry. The duck-footed table was neither old nor antique. She had bought it for Eighteenth Century on Second Avenue and had brought it proudly home with her in the station wagon, only to have David turn it upside down and scrape its bottom. It was as if he were scraping her own flesh. " I like it anyway," she'd said defiantly.

There must have been something about a duck-foot, for everybody liked it, including the mail lady. She was admiring it when Claudia returned to the living-room with Doctor and Mrs. Barry. The mail lady, separated from her dusty sedan, was like a snail without its shell. " Well, if it isn't Mrs. Naughton ! " she exclaimed, extending a limp hand with a quick little shake at the end of it. " Land sake, we're all certainly surprised to see you people selling out here. You could knock me over with a feather. Seems as if I sort of expected to keep on delivering mail to you people until I was old enough to be pensioned off—the place certainly won't be the same after you leave ; certainly seems you made up your mind in a big hurry."

" We did," said Claudia. " Like taking a dose of castor oil and having it over with." She'd always felt a professional respect for the mail lady, who used to honk her horn out front when there was a letter from David overseas. Now, off duty, and exposed in all her human frailties, she was not in the least formidable. " Certainly have had a hankering for this little table," she admitted. " I could see it through the window every time I drove past."

" It isn't a very good table." said Claudia, thinking that it certainly must have taken quite a lot of neck-craning to catch sight of it. " The one in the corner, though. really is old and fine." She pointed to a mahogany candlestand, limpid with age. The mail lady put up her nose. " Land sake, I got my house full of those kind," she said.

" So have I," said Mrs. Barry.

Their eyes locked in silent challenge. Eventually, the mail lady gave a nervous, untidy giggle. " No sense us bidding up against each other," she said.

" No sense in the least," Mrs. Barry agreed, clipping off a small, neat laugh, and all at once she got back to looking just the way she'd looked for the ten years that Claudia had known her. However, Dr. Barry seemed to know how to handle this end of her, too. " We have enough tables, Charlotte," he said firmly. " Come along, these people are busy."

He patted Claudia's shoulder. "Say hello to Matthew and Bobby for me. How's the city agreeing with them ? "

"Fine. Not even a cold so far." She reached for the mantel and knocked on it surreptitiously.

"And your husband ? Has he been having any more of those malaria attacks ? "

She kept on knocking. "Not lately, thank goodness. He's around, somewhere, waiting for Mrs. Riddle. I know he'll want to say good-bye to you."

"I'll find him," said Dr. Barry. He held out his hand. "Come back and see us occasionally. And take it easy for the next few months. Don't overdo."

"Well I declare," Mrs. Barry exclaimed, "I never could have told in a million years ! "

"I could." The mail lady gave a sly wink. "I thought to myself, ' Mrs. Naughton looks a teentsy-weentsy bit stouter.' Congratulations ! "

"Thank you," said Claudia, wincing at the teentsy-weentsy.

"Do you want a boy or a girl ? A girl, I guess, with two boys already." With an air of having settled the question, she picked up a green vase, glazed to the hilt. "This is darling, I love it. What'll it go for, I wonder ? "

"Not very much, it's only a vase from my appendix," said Claudia.

David came up in time to hear her say it. "You're a big help to Nancy," he remarked as he led her into the study to sign the deed.

"I bet all the trash will bring a fortune," she said gloomily.

"It always does. If we stayed around tomorrow, we could bid the good things back for almost nothing."

She brightened. "Should we ? "

"We should not," said David. "Let's cut clean."

Nancy was waiting for them. She had discarded her riding breeches for a baggy old suit and dreadful shoes. Nobody who wasn't very rich, Claudia decided, could afford to look so poor. She'd skipped her beauty-shop appointments, too. Her hair had grown out half-pink, half-white, and so had her nails, and little veins made up of weather and high blood pressure ran nakedly across her cheeks. The town clerk was waiting with her. He was nearly eighty, and looked fifty. Whenever Claudia had occasion to talk to him over the telephone, she always thought he was his wife, which was odd considering that he still ran a tractor and milked all his cows every day. Now he said with his high New England twang,

"Certainly sorry to lose you and your good husband from this community."

"We're sorry to go," said Claudia.

"Sign here," he said.

Claudia signed. David signed. Then Nancy signed, and the farm was sold.

TWO

MORE AND MORE people kept coming to look around. It reminded Claudia of the time they had the fire, when the whole town had turned out for the occasion. Cars drove up on the lawn from miles around, and children ate candy out of paper bags while they enjoyed the spectacle. Tomorrow would be a little like that. Unfamiliar labourers had already started to put up a lunch stand near the barn.

"There's no sense sticking around any longer," said David. "You look tired."

"Just a teentsy-weentsy bit," she allowed.

"How would you like a divorce ?·" said David.

He brought the car around to the front, while she washed up for the trip home. She sat down on the edge of the tub aware that her heart was thumping against her ribs. The day had been more of a strain than she had realized. She hoped it hadn't hurt the baby. In another few weeks she'd begin to feel life, which meant that she was quite a lot ahead of the game, inasmuch as she had found out only the month before that she was pregnant. Dr. Rowland, who had brought Bobby and Matthew and had taken care of her the last time, assured her that there was nothing to worry about, irregularities of that sort were apt to happen after a premature birth. "Still, you've got to be a little cautious," he had warned her.

Yes, she would be cautious. She was wiser now. She had thought that she could never lose a baby, but she had learned that anything could happen to anybody at any time.

She heard a light tapping at the window. Without turning, she knew that it was the big maple, brushing its branches against the pane. It was an aristocrat of trees, as beautiful in its dark brown winter habit as it was when it was decked with leaves. One day soon there would be snow, and every twig would be trimmed with white velvet, and if you saw it on a picture post card you wouldn't believe it. Claudia made that remark every winter, and David always agreed with her. It was one of the few remarks that could stand being said over and over.

It was hard to think that from this moment on the tree belonged to Nancy. Yet in a sense she would never own it, for though she might look at it, she wouldn't really see it.

Claudia left the bathroom with a feeling of guilt for taking the tree along with her.

She didn't tell David about it for fear he would think she was sentimental, but it was an odd coincidence that when they got home Matthew ran up to them demanding shrilly, "Did you sell the farm?" and David answered, "No, we brought it back with us."

Matthew was at an age when he put himself out to appreciate anything that sounded like a joke. "Where is it," he demanded with a loud hoot, "in your pocket?"

"Stupid," said Bobby, "Dad means he brought the farm back in his heart."

Impulsively Claudia put her arms around him and Bobby did not squirm away, much as he hated to be kissed. His cheek found hers, and for a moment they clung together. David ruffled their heads in a single caress. "Better get ready for supper," he said, clearing his throat.

Mary, who was Elizabeth's old cook and a very good one in a purely American way, was at her best with a prime rib roast. It was Bobby's favourite dish, especially when it was rare, with a great deal of red blood to spoon up around the platter. Tonight, however, he scarcely helped himself.

"What's the matter?" said Claudia. "Not even any gravy?"

"I'm not hungry," he said.

After supper he started off to bed without being prodded, and Claudia called him back to feel his forehead. "He's a little warm," she reported to David.

"Nonsense," said David. "This is a purely emotional thing with him."

She was willing to believe it, remembering the way she had felt that afternoon. "I wish we'd brought the dog and cat back with us," she said, speaking for herself. "It'd be less of a wrench for him."

"They'd have been too much for you to handle in the back seat," said David. "It's better for Edward to drop them off on his way to Jersey tomorrow."

"I suppose so," she acknowledged. "I hope the big city doesn't give Bluster a nervous breakdown."

"I hope so too," said David.

Bobby trailed in, only half undressed. "I want some cold ginger ale," he said without enthusiasm. "I'm thirsty."

"There's lots of water in the tap," Claudia said.

"Water doesn't taste good."

"That's tough luck," said David heartlessly. "What's taking you so long to go to bed?"

"I'm waiting for Matthew to get through."

"Get through, Matthew!" Claudia called in to Matthew.

"I am!" Matthew shouted back aggrieved. "I'm hurrying as fast as I can."

"He is not," said Bobby. "He's got a book."

David frowned. "How many times does he have to be told! That's a miserable habit."

"Don't look so virtuous," said Claudia. "Blood is thicker than water."

She found Matthew scrubbing his teeth with a great deal of fanfare. She eyed him coldly. "That's a completely dishonest gesture," she said. "I'll give you just two minutes to be in bed."

He made elaborate motions of haste, but in the end Bobby was in bed ahead of him, lying quietly, with his face to the wall. His cheeks were flushed, and Claudia was sure that he had been crying.

"Let him alone," David advised from over the newspaper. "He has a right to cry."

"I'm letting him alone," said Claudia. "I'm a lot older than he is, and it's hard even for me to cut loose."

He put the paper aside and glanced at his watch. "We still have time to make a theatre, if you want to."

"I don't, particularly. Unless you would?"

"No," said David. "I just thought perhaps you'd like to get your mind off."

"My mind's off. In fact I've got quite a sense of freedom all at once. No grass to cut or leaves to rake, milk delivered to the door, garbage taken away from the door, and a good school for the children around the corner. Also no trains to catch," she added, for his particular benefit.

"Yes'm," he said, with his eyes glued to the paper again.

"I think we did right to sell the place," said Claudia slowly.

"Yes'm."

"You're not listening."

"I am. You said we did right to sell the place."

"Aside from getting a good price, I mean."

"Still, it's a nice feeling to know that a good chunk of money is sitting in the bank."

"Provided," she remarked grimly, "that it doesn't sneak out into the stock market bit by bit."

He quickly turned the page he was reading, a little like

Matthew had brushed his teeth. " I don't know why you have that unholy prejudice to the market," he complained.

" Look at your brother's liver. That's why."

" Hartley speculates. Besides, his liver comes from Julia."

" What ails Julia comes from Hartley."

" Julia might go off half-cocked," he pointed out severely, " but she has a damn good business head. And it's high time that you learned something about investments too, young lady. Suppose I were to suddenly pop off. Then what ? "

" You sound like the Doctor's wife—' here today and gone tomorrow.' Any way, if there's any popping to be done, I'll be the one to do it."

" Nonsense. I'm seven years older. Also there are more widows than widowers, according to statistics."

" Oh hush." She put her hand over his mouth. " The only thing that's going to happen to you is that you're going to be frightfully successful and be sent to Iceland to build that radio station. That's why we didn't want to be tied to the farm. Remember ? "

He looked at his paper longingly. " Wouldn't you like to sit down and read a book, dear ? "

" I couldn't think of anything I'd like to do less, dear." She made a little face at him and walked to the window to watch a boat going by on the river. " This is a beautiful apartment," she sighed. " Much more expensive and luxurious than we could ever afford under ordinary circumstances. I hope it doesn't spoil me."

" See that it doesn't."

" I wonder will it be cool in summer ? "

" Wait until summer comes," he said.

She tried to think of next summer, but her thoughts wouldn't go that far. It was as if a curtain were dropped suddenly between the present and the future, suspending her in space. It was a little frightening not to be able to look forward. Coming back from the farm a black cat had darted in front of the car. People had silly ideas about black cats. Just the same, why did it have to pick out their car to cross in front of ?

She went over to David again and stood behind him, conquering the impulse to put her arms around him. He must have felt her need of him, for he threw aside the paper, and took her on his lap. Then he put the lamp out, and for a long while they sat quietly in the dark.

They might have gone on sitting there for hours if the door-bell hadn't rung. "Who can that be ? " they exclaimed in a single voice. New York wasn't like the country, people didn't drop in because they happened to be driving past and saw a light.

David turned on the lamp and blinked at his watch. "It's only ten past nine, it's probably John. He said if it wasn't too late when he left the office, he'd stop by with the mail."

"He's awfully reliable, isn't he ? "

"Reliable, and talented too. I have a great respect for him."

"Trade-last ! " Claudia waved to John as he came to the threshold.

"Hello," he said. "I hope I didn't wake you up or anything."

"No, we were only sitting," said Claudia. "Come on in."

He gave David a pile of mail and a roll of blueprints.

"There's nothing important here," David told him. "You could have saved yourself a trip."

"It was no trouble," said John. He smiled at Claudia. "What's my trade-last ? "

"What's mine ? "

"I hope I have the good luck to find a wife that's just like you."

"That's a handsome compliment," said Claudia. "Yours is that David just said you're going to be as famous an architect as he is some day."

"Don't believe a word of it," said David. He folded some papers and put them back in the envelope. "So the Cornwall people came down in their bid—sons-of-so-and-so's," he added with satisfaction.

John nodded. "All we have to do is sit tight, and they'll all come to their senses. Jason was in today about the shafts. I told him you'd be back at the office tomorrow. Did everything go all right at the farm ? "

"Yes," said David. "Want a highball ? "

"No, thanks." John sat down in a chair and stretched his long legs with an air of staying. "I hope I'm not keeping you up," he said. "Maybe I will have that highball."

David went out to the pantry. Claudia stifled a yawn. If John thought she was such a wonderful wife, she shouldn't be yawning at nine o'clock. John was sweet, but he wasn't very stimulating—not the way David was stimulating. Nevertheless, he had possibilities. He was the tall, gaunt type, interesting, as if he had the slightest touch of indigestion, which was rather distinguished in anyone under thirty, like premature white hair.

" Have you heard from Candy ? " he continued, swallowing his Adam's apple.

" Nothing, except that she'll be home sometime tomorrow for Thanksgiving. The children can't wait. You'd think she was their age."

" She's wonderful," said John, and suddenly his face became an open window to his heart. " He's in love with her," Claudia realized.

A few minutes later a key sounded in the latch, and Candy burst into their midst. John had known she was coming of course, and that's why he was there, not on account of any mail or blueprints.

They only shook hands, but even David saw at that moment how it was with them.

" This is a fine how-do-you-do," he said.

" Don't scold me," she implored. " I just had one class tomorrow, Greek, and I thought why wait for a silly thing like Greek, so here I am——"

" You should have let me meet you at the station," said John a little unsteadily.

" I didn't know until the last moment whether I was going to drive down with one of the girls—Claudia, you look blooming," she broke off deliriously, " and David got a new haircut ! "

" Wrong on the last one," said David. " I'm due at the barber's tomorrow."

Claudia decided that it must be the strain of selling the farm, for she had thought that Edward had had a haircut too. " Come on, darling," she said, " I'm tired, let's go to bed."

" She's tired, which means I have to go to bed," said David. " That's what getting married does to a man."

Candy and John looked at each other and laughed. " I won't stay too long," said John, as if anybody had asked him.

Candy followed them to their room. " It's wonderful to have you here to come home to." She kissed them both quickly, shyly. " Thanks for everything. I never thought I could be happy again. Do you think Mother minds my being happy ? "

" She'd mind dreadfully if you weren't," said Claudia.

" That's what I've been telling myself. Did you pass our house when you went to the farm ? Did it look neglected or overgrown ? "

"No," said David, "Edward's been keeping an eye on it. He got a couple of men in to rake the leaves and dig up the vegetables."

"Oh, that's good. Remind me to pay you."

"Very important," said Claudia, "with all of us camping here like this."

"I don't know what I'd do without you. Is Edward going to stay on with Nancy Riddle?"

"She wants him to, but he won't. He says he couldn't bear the place without us."

"Which is just the way I feel. I think we ought to sell our house too. With Mother gone, and you and David not there, I'll never use it. What's the point of holding on to it?"

"No point," David agreed. "Like the farm, it seems to have served its purpose."

"Nancy Riddle will buy it," said Claudia. "Nancy buys everything."

She spoke lightly but a sense of foreboding gripped her. One day, not too far away, Candy would be getting married, and David would be the first to say, "There's no point in your keeping this big apartment."

She mentioned something of the sort to him while they were undressing. "I hope Candy decides to remain single until after the baby comes—our baby I mean—or we'll be on the street."

"Nonsense," said David.

"You say 'nonsense' more than any man I ever knew."

"She's barely eighteen."

"I was only eighteen when I married Doctor," said Claudia. She sank down on Elizabeth's enormous double bed, revelling in every inch of it. "Mrs. Barry's a fool," she concluded. "Even if you do smoke."

THREE

DAVID FELL ASLEEP with his arm around her. She lay quietly, her eyes closed, but her mind awake. Candy's coming home stirred up so many memories. It seemed only yesterday that she had happened into their lives—a great overgrown girl of twelve, with her glands out of whack, and breasts too big for her legs. They had met for the first time in this very room, with Candy propped up in a chair getting over the measles. Claudia had brought her a book because Elizabeth was a new client and had just lost her husband, and David felt sorry for her.

In a way, it was all tangled up with the farm too, for Roger Killian, being David's senior partner and Elizabeth's cousin to boot, had wanted David to look at the detail of a fine old salt-box house in Eastbrook which they promptly bought the following autumn. Then Roger advised Elizabeth to build on a stretch of river land a few miles down the road, and Elizabeth had thought it would be a good thing for Candy. It was David who had drawn up the plans for the house—Roger was already getting less active in the firm—and even before they were neighbours, they had grown to be friends.

Eastbrook had not only done wonders for Candy, but Elizabeth's handling of her adolescent problems had been wise and unobtrusive. It was a big thing, Claudia reflected, for a woman to bring up a child without her husband. " Elizabeth was married just a little longer than David and I," it suddenly occurred to her with a tightening of her heart.

She wondered how there could be more than one great love in a woman's life. Perhaps there wasn't, perhaps you just passed that love along, as Elizabeth had done. It took courage for her to have married Jerry Seymour, younger than she and still groping toward a maturity he had never achieved. What a brief moment in space their marriage had been, as if she had paused on her way out of the world to bestow the meaning of love upon a confused and lonely soul. Poor Jerry. He had said, when he came home from the honeymoon in England alone, " I would rather have had those few short months with Elizabeth than a lifetime of living with any other woman." His saying that, and knowing that he meant it, was the one thing that had broken down Candy's passionate resentment of her

stepfather. "One of these days Jerry is going to write
a really great book," she said, "and it will be because of
Mother."

"I must ask Jerry to dinner during Candy's vacation,"
Claudia decided. She had a feeling that Elizabeth would like
it. She felt as if Elizabeth were quite close to her at this
moment. It was one of the few things that she and David
disagreed about. "When you're dead, you're dead," he always
insisted, and she couldn't make him admit that secretly he
had plenty of reason to believe otherwise.

"Why aren't you asleep ? " he murmured drowsily.

"I am," she said.

She was still awake when Bobby coughed—not a real cough
—just a swallow, probably, that had gone wrong. Glad to
have something to do, she crept out of bed and felt her way
through the dressing alcove that joined their rooms. He
seemed to take her being there for granted. "It's cold," he
said, without bothering to open his eyes.

"No wonder ; you kicked the blankets on the floor." She
tucked them up around his chin ; his legs fought them
restlessly. "It's too hot," he complained.

"Well, make up your mind, sonny," she retorted, but immediately she was suspicious of this hot and cold business.
"I don't want to have my temperature taken," he anticipated
her.

She added injury to insult when she told him to turn over.

"That's Matthew's thermometer ! " he protested. "That's
for babies ! "

"Don't be silly. Any baby can put it in his mouth," she
said.

The small of his back gave up a flame of heat. Her knees
buckled. When would she learn not to get panicky when the
children were ill ? Would she ever learn ?

"It's finished," he whimpered.

"Now come on now, lie still, it's not half a minute yet."

"It is so." His lips quivered. "I don't want you to go
out."

She humoured him. "Do I look as if I were going out in
the middle of the night in my bathrobe ? "

"Tomorrow, I mean. Don't go out, you're always going
out."

"That's a whopper ; I'm the least going-out mother you'll
ever have."

"You go to Aunt Julia's for dinner."

" So that's what you're holding against me—because once —just once, mind you, since we've been in New York, we went to a party at Aunt Julia's. Why, you little I-don't-know-what ! "

She waited anxiously for the sheepish grin which badinage always brought to his lips, but there was no smiling in him now. " You always go away and leave us," he insisted in a feverish singsong.

" When ? " she demanded indignantly. " Where ? "

" You went away to be an actress on the stage for a whole year."

" A month. It only seemed like a year. And anyway, I have that all out of my system," she assured him. " And something else in," she added, which was safe because he didn't know about the baby yet.

" I hurt," he whimpered. " I hurt all over. I want some ginger ale."

Her heart reproached her with a sick thud against her ribs. He had wanted ginger ale before he went to bed, and he hadn't eaten any supper, and both she and David had thought it was emotional. There was nothing emotional about this. She held the thermometer beneath the lamp, but even before she looked at it closely, she could see that the slim thread of mercury had darted frighteningly toward the top of the stick.

A sound from the bed made her turn. Bobby suddenly looked pinched and green around the nostrils. Once Matthew had a convulsion. Children sometimes had them with high fever. Panic exploded in her brain. Whom could she call ? She didn't know any doctors in New York—— If only Doctor Barry were here.

" Don't get excited, he's all right," said David's voice behind her. He moved her aside and took her place. " Quick, get a basin——"

She ran for a basin.

" It's just something he ate," said David. " Lie back, Bobby, take it easy, you'll feel better now."

Bobby lay back, his breath quick and shallow with exhaustion, his eyes luminous with fever. The flush was back upon his cheeks again, and he looked unearthly and beautiful, as children sometimes did when they were very ill. He had been as sentient about the farm, Claudia remembered, as if he had been lifted to some rarefied height of understanding.

" Oh darling——"

" Don't ' darling ' him," said David brusquely. " How many peanuts did you eat, Bobby ? "

Bobby seemed not to hear. He lay inert, with his face away from them. " Don't think this can't be psychic too," said David argumentatively.

" With over 103 ? "

" People get blind and paralysed from psychic disturbances."

For all his fancy ideas, though, she could see that he didn't believe that this was an emotional upset because he followed up by saying, " If you're going to worry all night, call the doctor."

" What doctor ? "

" New York is full of them."

" But we don't know any."

" Candy must know somebody."

There was a light in the living-room. John hadn't gone home yet. He was standing by the fireplace, and Candy was sitting on the sofa. Her eyes were almost as luminous as Bobby's. She smiled apologetically when she saw them. " John's going in a minute, I'm coming right to bed."

John said, " I didn't realize it was so late. What time is it ? "

" Bobby's sick," said Claudia. " What doctor did your mother have for you, Candy ? "

" Dr. Grannis. But he's dead. He was killed in the war."

It was strange how every once in a while the war came back. Her hand reached for David's. She felt his fingers alive and strong around her own. What would she ever do without him ?

" Don't you know anyone else ? " David asked.

Candy shook her head. " We haven't needed anybody. Except Doctor Barry in the summers for poison oak and things like that."

" We have a good man," said John, " only he's in Greenwich."

" That won't help."

" It's too bad about the youngster. Gosh, I'm sorry."

" I'm devastated," said Candy.

They meant it, but they really didn't know what it was like to have a sick child. They were at the sweet commencement of their love, they were yet to taste its bitter richness.

John came up with another suggestion. " What about asking your sister-in-law ? "

" Julia always has Doctor Rowland," said Claudia. " He's

chiefly good for women." It was through Julia that she herself had first gone to Dr. Rowland, for which he had small reason to be grateful, since she had turned out to be not only a poor relation but a persistently pregnant one in the bargain. It would be putting salt on a wound to call him for Bobby, who was ten years removed from any possible interest Dr. Rowland might have had in him.

David looked at his watch. "We'll phone Julia anyway, she's bound to know somebody else."

The butler answered—Julia was back in full and foreign staff again since the war. The butler said with Austrian preciseness, "Mrs. Naughton is at the opera. I will see if Mr. Naughton is at home. Who is calling, please ? "

" Mr. Naughton's brother," said Claudia.

" He must think Mr. Naughton's brother is a pretty queer guy," said David, with an effort to be funny.

When Hartley finally got to the telephone, he sounded as if he had been in the middle of something or other—once in a while he befriended young actresses or singers and helped them along. His voice was almost guilty with cordiality. He said it was too bad about Bobby, always something the matter with children, but it probably was nothing to worry about. So they'd really sold the farm ? Fine. Fine. In his opinion, they were smart not to put it off, this was a buyer's market. Well, now that they were back in civilization, they all ought to have dinner one of these evenings, go to the theatre, see a bit of the old town together. Oh yes—a doctor—well now, there was Kirkland, Janeway, and Stratter. Neissen, but he wouldn't do. All splendid men, fine men, but specialists, unfortunately.

Claudia didn't have to ask what kind of specialists, since she had learned most of Hartley's diseases by heart: gall bladder, hypertension, prostate and a periodic rash along his stomach.

In the end she thought of the little doctor on the ground floor that they had called in some emergency the winter they'd rented a furnished apartment in New York. Thereafter he had gratefully attended them at any hour of the day or night, and had been sorry when they went back to Eastbrook.

" He was very thorough," Claudia recalled. " We had him for Matthew several times, and he diagnosed my appendix. I think his name was Marks. No, Mack."

David looked him up in the telephone book, running his finger down the MACKS.

"Leo! That's the one," Claudia broke in, "and he has his office and home together on West Seventy-first Street, I think it was."

"This 'Leo' seems to have his office on Park Avenue, and lives on East Sixty-third Street."

"Oh dear," said Claudia. "Let's take a chance, anyway, and see if he's the same."

He was the same, but in name only, so to speak. He had not only moved to the East side, but he now had an assistant who took care of his late calls, unless the case was urgent.

Claudia assured him that the case was most urgent and added, for good measure, that she was one of his old patients. It wasn't so smart to remind him, because he froze up a little, as if he didn't want to remember old patients. However, when she gave him Elizabeth's Beekman Place address, he froze down again and said that he would leave his guests and run in to take a look at Bobby.

He appeared twenty minutes later. Although he wore a new manner and a dinner jacket, he was basically very little different from when he had had his office on the West side. He glanced around the living-room appraisingly—not knowing it was Elizabeth's—and remembered Claudia's appendix immediately. "You know, of course, that I haven't been in general medicine since the war," he mentioned, "I'm a nose and throat specialist."

"But aren't there any specialists in general medicine any more?" Claudia asked. "It makes you feel so unsafe with children."

"Certainly," he said. "I can refer you to an excellent pediatrician."

He followed them to Bobby's room. Bobby cringed at the touch of the chilly stethoscope against his chest. Claudia remembered how Dr. Barry always warmed the metal against the palm of his hand, and how he'd say something cheerful before he put the instrument away like, "Clear as a bell," or "You'll live, young man."

Dr. Mack made no comment other than that he couldn't be sure what the boy was developing. "From the present symptoms," he said, "it could be a number of things. I'll know more tomorrow when we see what his temperature does. If his fever goes down, well and good. If it doesn't——" Dr. Mack snapped his bag shut. "At any rate, I'll be here at nine."

Toward dawn Claudia stole to Bobby's side for the dozenth

time. He was asleep, but his eyes were not fully closed. It was terrifying to see a child asleep with his eyes half shut. She touched her lips to his temples. His skin was scorching. His fever hadn't gone down, he was hotter than he had been all night. Fear rose up in her like some mammoth invasion of her being, choking her throat and causing her to become weak and dizzy. She steadied herself against the bedpost, aware that the new life within her was drawing upon her strength. In a flash of terror it came to her that perhaps God was giving her one child so that He could take another from her. Perhaps she had more than her share of happiness in a world so full of suffering. Often this crazy feeling came to her ; it was as if her very blessings were hanging over her head like a sword.

She did not know David was at her side until he spoke. "Stop imagining things," he said in a gruff, matter-of-fact voice that was like a strong arm around her.

"His fever's much higher."

David put his hand on Bobby's forehead.

"Say ' nonsense,' " she prayed. But he took his hand away again and said, " It'll probably be down in the morning."

By seven, however, Bobby's temperature had climbed to a hundred and four and two-tenths, whereupon David finally delivered himself of a belated " nonsense," and proclaimed that it was only a hundred and four. It was such a small, sweet lie that she didn't argue with him. As if two-tenths of a degree, one way or another, could change the fact that Bobby was very sick.

"There's nothing you can do about it until the doctor comes," David continued sensibly, " so go back to bed, and I'll ask Mary to bring you breakfast on a tray."

" I wouldn't leave him alone."

" What do you think he'll do, get up and dance a jig ? "

" I wish he felt like it. I couldn't look at breakfast, I'm not hungry."

" That's no way to act in your delicate condition."

" My delicate condition will have to get along by itself," she said. " I can't be bothered with it now." She wanted to add that one in the hand was worth two in the bush, but the lump in her throat wouldn't let her say it.

Bobby stirred and tried to get up. " I have to go out in the barn to help Edward feed the cows," he cried out in the loud, passionless voice of delirium.

David replaced the blanket over his thrashing limbs.

" Stay covered like a good boy. You'll get up when you feel better. How about a little drink of water ? "

" Ginger ale," Bobby murmured through parched lips. " With lots of ice."

" I'll get it," said Claudia.

She was glad that David had not reminded him that the farm had been sold, nor held out in its place the promise of new adventures. Bobby had been wildly excited about the prospect of going to Iceland, but now that he was ill, the familiar surroundings of home seemed to fill a deeper need. It was just as well that he did not realize that he had no home at this point. Elizabeth's apartment offered them a temporary haven, but it could not possibly spell permanence on a scale of living so far beyond David's drawing account. They could afford the upkeep of two maids merely because they paid practically no rent.

Mary and Katie, immaculate in crisp morning uniforms, were already in the kitchen. Elizabeth had trained her servants faultlessly, and her death had not interrupted the smooth running of her household. They both liked children, and didn't mind a new one, but whether their serene good humour would survive the imminent arrival of a Great Dane dog and a gigantic Persian cat remained to be seen. " I don't so much care for cats, but I like little dogs," Mary had remarked doubtfully. " Miss Candy always had a Scottie." Bluster was no Scottie.

At the moment they were deeply concerned to hear that Bobby had taken sick during the night. " There's a lot of mumps around," said Mary. " You'd best be careful, Mrs. Naughton, and not be after catching anything, it wouldn't be good at all."

" Parents don't catch from their children," said Claudia.

" Oh yes, they do," Mary maintained. " My sister's brother-in-law just got the mumps from his five-year-old son, and it's no joke, that it's not. He's got a trained nurse even."

" Mumps are something special," Claudia explained. " Especially with men. Anyway Bobby's had them. So's Matthew. Also measles, chicken pox, and scarlatina."

" Then there's nothing to fret about," Katie inserted, " as long as they've had most everything."

It was more than ever the cause to fret. By a subtle process of elimination, Dr. Mack had hinted of poliomyelitis, mastoids, and pneumonia.

Candy was hovering in the hall outside of Bobby's room when

Claudia returned with the ginger ale. She couldn't help being suddenly conscious of her heavy-eyed pallor against Candy's sleepy young loveliness ; her body felt lumpy and heavy in the serviceable flannel robe that she always kept by her bed in case the children needed her at night. She wondered that Candy did not feel the early chill through the thin silk of her peppermint-stripe pyjamas.

" David doesn't want me to go in the room until we know what Bobby has," she whispered. " Isn't there anything I can do ? "

" Yes, run put something warm on, and see that Matthew gets dressed. Bertha can take him right off to kindergarten as soon as she comes."

" I'll take him," Candy offered eagerly. " You keep Bertha here, you'll need her."

" Thanks," said Claudia.

It was an added luxury to have Bertha living in the neighbourhood. It was good for Bertha too. She couldn't leave Fritz for too long at a time, so she was glad to have a few hours work a day. Claudia couldn't help feeling a little guilty at not having to lift a finger when it came to either the children or the house. " I'm spoiled as can be," she told David. " Do you realize that all of a sudden, I'm keeping two-and-a-half in help ? "

" It's coming to you," he replied. " I'm enjoying every minute of it."

FOUR

THIS MORNING, as if she sensed trouble, Bertha appeared much earlier than her usual time. "I did not like the way Bobby acted yesterday in the park," she admitted. "He was very quiet, but no fever, so I thought maybe it was because he was sorry about the farm."

"So did we," said Claudia. She watched Bertha's face as she stood by Bobby's bed and studied his miserable little body with knowing eyes. "What do you think it is ? "

"Just a cold," Bertha decided. "Everybody gets bad colds in New York when the winter begins."

"Exactly," said David, appearing like a nicely scented breeze. He was shaved and dressed, with a fresh point of view, and ready to go into cahoots with Bertha at the drop of a hat.

"If you're so sure of it," Claudia challenged him, "why are you waiting around for the doctor instead of going to the office ? "

"To give you moral support. I never saw anyone go to pieces like you do."

"I didn't either," she acknowledged meekly. "I could kick myself for it."

She left Bertha in charge while she popped into a tub and out again—she was never one to make a great to-do about a bath. Matthew walked in as she was wrapping herself in a towel. "It's polite to knock," she informed him.

He was neither curious nor observant. "Is Bobby going to die ? " he demanded with a much livelier interest.

"Matthew, be quiet, what a thing to say ! "

"People who get very sick always die," Matthew insisted sagely. "Aunt Elizabeth died, and I saw a dead cat on the street on my way to kindergarten yesterday. When is Edward bringing Shakespeare ? "

"This afternoon."

"Bluster too ? "

"Yes."

"Is Edward going to live here with us like on the farm ? "

"No."

"Why not ? Don't you like Edward ? "

"Yes."

" Then why doesn't he live here ? "

" Because we have no cows to take care of. Now run along to breakfast."

" I had it already. I had orange juice and toast and oatmeal. Why do I have to have oatmeal all the time," he paused to resent.

" You don't have it all the time."

" I had to have farina yesterday and that's the same thing."

" It isn't the same thing," Claudia told him shortly. " Matthew please—get ready for school, you're going with Candy. Come back, button your fly——"

He was really getting to be a big boy, she reflected—fly and all. He was like Bobby at that age. She remembered how Bobby had always hated to go to school with a sense of insecurity clouding his day. It was wrong not to have sent him off with an easier mind. She could scarcely wait for Candy to come back to find out whether he seemed upset.

" Upset ? He was happy as a lark," said Candy. " He hasn't reached the stage where he tunes in."

" I hope for his sake he never does."

" So do I. I used to suffer like anything when I was a child."

Claudia had to smile. In spite of Candy's concern and sympathy, she was finding it excessively difficult to tune into unhappiness this morning. She still carried in her eyes the glow of last night's reunion with John, and for a moment of escape Claudia savoured the glorious idiocy of new love. She knew how Candy had wakened to the instant joy of knowing that he was in the world with her, how her thoughts were running through her mind like a bright ribbon, weaving his image. Candy was suspended in space, waiting for the sound of his voice over the telephone ; Claudia was suspended in space, too, waiting for Dr. Mack.

She blessed him for being prompt to the minute of nine o'clock. What he lacked in inspiration, he compensated for with a high degree of organization. Meticulously, he arranged his instruments on a white towel on the table, before he started to use them—stethoscope, tongue-depressor, ear-light, and dilator. Claudia watched him in sheer torture, for Bobby's symptoms had begun to localize with alarming implication. During the past hour he had complained of a sore throat, a stiff neck, and a pain in his toes. The neck frightened her. but the toes threw her off a little. When Dr. Mack finally got around to examining him, however, it was the toes and not

the neck that became the pivotal factor in his diagnosis.
"This looks like the grippe," he announced, as one by one he
carefully wiped his instruments and put them back in his
satchel.

Claudia felt giddy with the load of relief that rolled off her
mind. "Is that all ? " she exclaimed happily.

"The grippe is not to be taken lightly," Dr. Mack reproved
her.

"What I meant was," she explained, "I'm so grateful it's
not poliomyelitis or pneumonia."

Dr. Mack allowed her to be grateful with an air of continu-
ing disapproval. He dried his small clean hands on a lacy
guest towel. "I shall leave a prescription which you will
pleased have filled at once. Give one powder every three
hours while the temperature remains above a hundred and
one. And remember," he added portentously, "the grippe
can have serious, even fatal results if not carefully watched
and held in check."

David barely waited until the door had closed on Dr. Mack's
departing back. "What a pompous calamity howler," he
expostulated.

"I knew all the time it was only a cold," said Bertha with
complacence.

Bobby went into violent contortions when he took the
powder, but an hour or so later his temperature dropped as if
by magic, and also, as if by magic, he began to lose the angelic
aura of extreme illness. "I want some ginger ale," he
demanded.

"You'll take cold water and like it," said Claudia, also losing
the aura.

He regarded her in wounded astonishment. She hugged
him hard. "You good-for-nothing, I could wring your neck.
You scared the wits out of me."

She ate an enormous lunch—enough for three—after which
Bertha marched her into her room to lie down. "Bobby is
all right, so now you please look after the baby," she
instructed.

"That leaves Matthew unprovided for," Claudia demurred.
She crossed her fingers. "I only hope he doesn't get the cold.
Though maybe he had his share with his blood poisoning last
summer."

"Sickness does not work like that," said Bertha. "The
more run down you are the more you get."

"Like money," said Claudia. "And children."

It was hard to be popped into bed, willy nilly, in the middle of the day. No wonder Matthew always kicked about his afternoon rest. Candy's step in the hall a few minutes later offered a welcome diversion. "Candy," she called, "come here and keep me company!"

Candy appeared with her coat slung over her shoulders and a beret stuck on the back of her head. "Oh," said Claudia, "I didn't know you were going out."

"Not really out. Bertha wants me to call for Matthew at school and take him straight to the park to keep him away from Bobby. And buy him a malted milk please, not a soda, no matter how he begs. Bertha's priceless."

"She doesn't care what she does to your vacation, does she?"

"She knows I adore anything that has to do with the children."

Claudia regarded Candy affectionately. "You remind me of one of those fashion pictures," she said, "'what the teen-agers are wearing.'"

"Is that supposed to be a compliment?"

"I wish someone would say it to me."

"I think you're beautiful. So does David."

Claudia made a face. "Beautiful like in the Bible."

"Lots of women aren't," said Candy. "They look awful." She sighed enviously. "I'd trade anything I've got for your hair. All you have to do is run a comb through it and you're fixed." Candy looked gloomy as she contemplated an awkward future. "I can just see me if I ever get married, sprouting curlers all over my head like a porcupine every night."

That indeed, Claudia conceded, was a grim outlook. Thank goodness that she didn't have to take herself to pieces for a general overhauling before she went to bed with David. "But you could always get a permanent," she suggested.

"I kink," said Candy. "To look right, I have to be practically straight except for the ends."

Candy was certainly wearing her heart on her sleeve. Up to the time she had met John, she had gone around with a pigtail behind each ear, not caring how she looked. Now her slim, long-legged loveliness proclaimed to the world that she was in love. David, in some strange way, had prepared her for that love. Claudia remembered with a flush of shame, how she had been afraid after Elizabeth's death that he was

responding to Candy's desperate need of affection and understanding. She could not have foretold the benign pattern of
their whole relationship.

"Claudia," Candy's voice broke into her musings.
"Claudia, listen, I have something to ask you, and please be
perfectly frank about it."

"Since when am I not ? "

"This is different. You'll probably say ' yes ' just to be nice."

"Come to the point."

"You sounded like mother just then. Well anyway,
tomorrow's Thanksgiving."

Claudia's hand reached for Candy's. "I know. Holidays
—for the first year or two at least—are pretty awful."

"Especially Thanksgiving." Candy had to swallow before
she went on. "We never had a turkey. Nor a big dinner
like most people. Neither mother nor I liked turkey particularly—we always let Mary and Katie go off to their own
family dinners, and we'd fix something for ourselves.
Lobster, usually, or a rarebit. It was awfully right, somehow.
I mean, Thanksgiving is a sort of a private thing, like getting
married. I always told mother I'd never want a big wedding,
and she always said, good for me."

"I say ' good for you,' too. David and I didn't have anyone
at our wedding except my mother and Hartley and Julia. It
was all the relatives we had left between us."

"John has loads of relatives," said Candy, giving herself
away completely. "They believe in big families and lots of
holidays and simply huge turkeys, so John thought that it
would be a nice change if I'd drive out to Greenwich with him
tomorrow and have dinner at his house."

"I think it's a wonderful idea."

"Do you really ? I was afraid you and David might think
the least I could do was to stay home."

"Actually we do," said Claudia. "The minute your back
is turned we're going to talk about you."

Candy giggled. Then her face grew grave. "Mother would
like John, don't you think ? "

"Yes, I do."

"David must like him too, or he wouldn't have him in the
office."

"David's devoted to him."

"And John idolizes David, that goes without saying. People
liking each other makes them seem to belong together,
doesn't it ? "

Claudia nodded. Candy was trying to put into words the strange pattern of their closeness.

"The one thing that bothers me," Candy continued, "is that John's only being nice to me on account of David. I mean, every so often he starts treating me like a younger sister."

"After all, he is eight years older than you are," Claudia pointed out sensibly.

"Seven. It's only eight for a couple of months a year. It's the same difference as between you and David, isn't it ? "

"About," Claudia admitted.

There was a small pause, during which Candy sat floating in bliss. After a moment she rose. "Then you're sure you don't mind about tomorrow ? "

"Sure," said Claudia.

Candy drifted off, walking on air. "Don't get run over ! " Claudia called after her.

A few minutes later, Julia came. "I just met Candy downstairs," she said. "Or rather, she bumped into me." Julia laughed. "I still don't think the child knew me, her head was in the clouds, somewhere."

"I know," said Claudia. "It's wonderful."

Julia raised her slender brows. "John ? "

"How did you guess ? "

Julia laughed. "A little bird told me there was going to be a wedding very soon."

"Your little bird is only half-right. Candy has to finish college, and John's just getting on his feet, professionally."

Julia laughed again. "We'll see," she said. "At any rate, it'll be a good marriage. They're both of excellent family."

"Is that so important ? " Claudia enquired mildly.

"It helps." Julia loosened her sable stole, emitting her usual little gust of expensively subtle perfume. "Hartley told me when I came home last night that Bobby was ill. I'm glad he's all right again."

Claudia wondered why Julia, who was usually very attentive to her in-laws, hadn't telephoned that morning to find out about him, instead of waiting until mid-afternoon. Probably, though, she'd called David earlier—she and David were having a lot to say to each other these days about the stock-market—Julia's flair for the market being the one thing about her that he ever had a kind word for. "How does it feel," she continued now, running true to form, "to have all that money from the sale of the farm sitting prettily in cash ? "

"Fine," said Claudia. "I only hope," she added pointedly, "that David lets it sit there."

"I only hope he doesn't," Julia replied with asperity. "The market's booming."

"I'd rather it boomed without us," said Claudia. "I'd rather have less and know we've got it."

"That's ridiculous," said Julia. "Particularly when the only way you can keep anything these days is through Capital Gains."

Julia always spoke as if Capital Gains were some great benefactor to the human race. "Also," she continued severely, "suppose you had a big rent to pay ? You'd find it pretty difficult to live this way on what David draws."

"We wouldn't live this way," said Claudia cheerfully.

"Incidentally," Julia digressed, "what'll you do if Candy wants the apartment when she's married ? I don't see how she can help herself, with places so impossible to find."

"I've thought of that, and it's the one thing that worries me. It's a new experience to have no roots, to say nothing of no roof."

Julia gave one of those small secret smiles so full of knowing. "I wouldn't fret about it," she said.

"Why shouldn't I fret," Claudia demanded, "with the baby due in April ? " It was as if Julia had got her all set to worry and then told her it was a false alarm.

"Well, go on and worry," said Julia, "if it makes you feel better. But I promise you, you'll have a roof over your heads. Of course, it might only be an igloo—or do they have igloos in Iceland ? "

So that was it—Julia had found out something about David's commission, and was trying to tell her without really telling her. Hartley probably knew a director—Hartley always knew directors—and although David would be wild at the idea of any pressure being brought to bear, Claudia wasn't so particular. "How do you know ! " she cried excitedly. "Who told you ? Tell me ! "

Julia shook her head, tantalizing and mysterious. "I'm afraid you won't believe it."

"I will ! "

"I've just come from a sitting," said Julia. "'V' came through very powerfully."

"Oh," said Claudia, and almost added one of David's most expressive comments. "So that's the little bird that's too busy telling you things," she remarked instead.

" Don't scoff," said Julia softly. " I know I shouldn't have said anything about it. I knew you wouldn't understand."

Claudia stared at her incredulously. What a strange mixture of horse sense and nonsense Julia had become. She had always dabbled a little in fortune-telling and astrology, but not more so than most people with time and money on their hands. Then the war came, and Julia had been busy winning it ; then the war stopped, and Julia's energies had been released with a bang, and all at once she went into spiritualism, as some people go into religion. It wasn't as if she had a lot of friends and relatives on the other side—to talk to either. It was a much more personal thing than that, Julia had struck up a passionate intimacy with a perfectly strange spirit she'd never laid eyes on in real life. As far as Claudia could gather from Julia's guarded confidences, this spirit, who called himself " V," with a stark and impressive austerity, was an Arab and a physician. He had also, Julia once let drop very tremulously, been her husband long centuries past in another life.

Out of sheer decency and an abiding affection toward her sister-in-law for all the birthday and Christmas presents she had lavished upon them throughout the years, Claudia had refrained from mentioning the relationship to David. However, if he showed any signs of taking Julia's advice about the stock market, she made up her mind on the spot that she would have no further qualms about it. Julia was undoubtedly showing signs of climacteric deterioration, and David had better realize that her counsel was not to be trusted.

" I've never felt ' V's ' vibration to be as strong as today," Julia continued dreamily, " and somehow or other, your vibration seemed to be very strong too." She smiled faintly. " My nose was quite out of joint ; he spent most of my precious time talking about your affairs."

" That was very nice of him," said Claudia. It was on the tip of her tongue to assure Julia that she had no cause for jealousy, but it would have been cruel to make fun of her. In a way, Julia was as much in love as Candy, and one didn't make fun of people in love. It was certainly an indictment of Hartley, Claudia reflected, that his wife should be running after a man who had been dead for hundreds of years.

" How did you happen to tell ' V ' about the Iceland project in the first place ? " she asked.

It was a catch question, worthy of David, but Julia was not to be caught. " I didn't tell him, he told me. He said,

'Someone who is very close to you, will be going off into a cold climate, and for a time you will be lonely and distraught.' "

Claudia had noticed that "V's" messages had a tendency to assume poetic cadence, and the "lonely and distraught" part was a little far fetched, considering that Julia wouldn't be apt to miss her in-laws to that extent. Still, it was very nice of her not to deny it. "We'll write to you," Claudia promised lightly.

Julia sat forward, her thin patrician face intense and devoted. "You really don't believe at all, do you?" she said in a low voice.

"I believe in life after death," Claudia admitted. "I often feel that Mamma's very close to me, but I don't need anybody to go in a trance to tell me about it."

"I don't subscribe to the average medium either," Julia readily agreed. "The best of them resort to trickery. But 'V' is different," she went on unsteadily. "You know me well enough to know that I'm the most stable, hard-headed person in the world——"

"You used to be," Claudia amended silently.

"But I can't refute undeniable proof," Julia concluded. "Not evidence, mind you. But proof."

Claudia asked what the difference was, and Julia explained at great length that evidence was one thing and proof was another, but it all sounded the same to Claudia. She lay back on her pillow, listening, but not hearing. Her hand rested gently upon her abdomen. She was a universe unto herself.

"Did 'V' say whether I was going to have a boy or a girl?" She couldn't resist finding out.

"I didn't ask him," said Julia. "He did say though, that there was illness, but it would be all right. That's how I knew that Bobby was better, you see."

"It's almost as good as having a doctor in the family," said Claudia.

"It is," Julia agreed seriously. "'V' read Hartley's last X-rays. He described the condition of the gall bladder perfectly, and said that Hartley should *not* be operated on."

"I didn't know he was going to be," said Claudia. "I thought he was."

"He's not," said Julia.

"Oh," said Claudia blankly.

Clearly they had reached an impasse. Claudia was glad for the interruption of Bobby's voice, loud and swaggering with feeling better. " Hey, who is that in there ? " he demanded. " Why don't people come in and see me ! "

" People will," Julia called back.

She stood a discreet distance from his bed, because she was subject to colds. " Hello, young man," she said.

" Hello," said Bobby back, trying not to show that he noticed she hadn't brought him anything.

" Feeling better ? " she asked.

" Yes," he said.

Conversation languished. Julia was full of dutiful affection for Bobby and Matthew, but she was not running over with maternal instinct. It was a relief to all of them when the door-bell rang, and suddenly a single thunderous bark reverberated through the walls. " Bluster's here ! " Bobby shouted, bouncing up in excitement.

" Lie down and stay covered," Claudia said. " I'll bring him in to you."

She emerged into the lounge to see Edward come flying through the front door at the end of Bluster's leash like a comic strip. " Take your time, what's the rush ! " she expostulated, mistaking Bluster's horizontal progression for delight.

" Watch out, Mrs. Naughton ! " Edward warned.

Claudia had sufficient experience to duck, but Julia came out of Bobby's room and didn't know enough to get out of the way. In a frenzy of panic and confusion, Bluster reared up on his hind legs and threw his great front paws around her immaculate shoulders for protection. Julia was not the screaming kind, but she screamed, and Mary, who had trustfully opened the door, and who was now cowering against the wall, screamed in sympathy.

The screams unnerved Bluster completely. He collapsed to the floor and scrabbled across the slippery expanse of waxed wood, making a hash of the rugs and knocking over a small table. Eventually he reached a temporary haven behind the living-room sofa, and again fell in a heap. " You frightened him," Claudia explained to Julia, a trifle reproachfully.

Julia's eyes widened as if she had not heard correctly. She opened her lips to speak, but her voice was gone. A moment later, she was gone too.

" I want to see Bluster ! " Bobby kept shrieking.

" I wouldn't if I was you, Mrs. Naughton," Edward advised in half-tones. He mopped his forehead and glanced at Bluster apprehensively. Bluster was still lying behind the couch, his massive head hidden beneath his paws on the theory that if he could not see anybody, nobody could see him. "I let him stay downstairs for a good while before I brought him up," Edward enlarged with delicacy, "but I guess he was too excited."

"Oh, I imagine he'll last a little longer," said Claudia optimistically.

FIVE

WHEN DAVID CAME HOME from the office, Bluster was still lasting, and Claudia was on pins and needles. " I wouldn't play with him too roughly," she suggested, " until you take him out again."

Sometime later David sat down to a ruined dinner. " The traffic seems to make him tongue-tied," he reported briefly.

" We'll both go out with him next trip," said Claudia. " Maybe that's what he wants."

From the farthest corner of the dining-room Bluster rolled his eyes without lifting his head.

" He said ' yes,' " Claudia interpreted, but it turned out to be " no."

" You go to bed," said David. " I'll sit up and read a couple of hours, and try it again."

" I'll sit up with you. I never can go to sleep anyway until you're in bed too."

" That's a bad habit," he lashed out at her out of a clear sky, " and very annoying to a man."

" I don't like it any more than you do," she assured him coldly.

It was long past midnight when they both finally climbed beneath the covers. " We might have been in bed hours ago," Claudia grumbled, " for all the good it did us to wait up. Do you think he's just stubborn, or what ? "

" What," said David lucidly.

They were almost asleep when she remembered to tell him about Julia. " David," she whispered. " Are you awake ? "

His head popped up like a Jack-in-the-box. " I didn't hear him——"

" Oh lie down," she said impatiently. " This is something more important than Bluster's bladder."

" There's nothing more pressing that I can think of at the moment."

" No ? Well what would you say if I were to tell you that you were going to get the Iceland commission ? "

" Very nice," he said, pretending he didn't care.

" So you don't want to know how I know ? " Claudia teased him. " Julia told me."

He reminded her of Bobby, the way he tried not to be interested. " And who told Julia, may I ask ? "

" ' V '," said Claudia.

He began to sense foul play. " Who the hell is ' V ' ? " he growled.

" Julia's first husband," said Claudia. " He's been dead five hundred years."

It sounded so outlandish that he didn't pay any attention to her, much less believe her. He gave a grunt and humped the quilt over his shoulder, and rudely rolled away from her.

" You'll be sorry when the stock market drops," she threw after him.

He was awake at six and tried to steal out of bed. She caught him by the coat of his pyjamas. " Fat chance, come back, I looked at Bobby a little while ago. He was all right."

" It's not Bobby I'm worried about. I'd better take the dog out."

" You never got up at this hour to put your children on the pottie," she remarked.

" My children weren't as big."

There was something in what he said. If Bluster were a Pomeranian, they might just let the whole thing rest with Nature. As it was, there was no telling what had happened in the middle of the night. She fished for her mules, and followed him.

They tiptoed through the hall, peering anxiously around, and eventually found Bluster in the pantry, dreaming in gusts that shook his jowls and quivered his whiskers. " Don't disturb him," David whispered, " until I get some clothes on."

" I'll get dressed and go with you."

" What for ? "

" Company."

" I don't feel sociable," said David.

" You didn't last night either," she accused him. " This is ruining our marriage."

She killed time while they were gone by trying to locate Shakespeare. " I don't know where you've disappeared to, but you're a gentleman and a scholar," she addressed the pan of paper in the bathroom. She got down on her hands and knees and looked under all the furniture. A pair of yellow searchlights gleamed through the darkness beneath the ruffle of the sofa. She reached out and almost captured a velvet paw, only to have it melt away to her touch. " Don't be coy," she adjured him shortly.

It was a battle of wits and persistence, and finally she dragged him out. He hung limply in her arms, a sullen burden of orange fur. They stared at each other. "This is silly," said Claudia, and dropped him.

He agreed that it was silly, and walked off with his tail sticking up in the air. "In case I forgot to tell you to your face," she called after him, "you're a pleasure next to a certain dog I know ! "

She brushed her teeth and combed her hair, and still it was only half-past six. She thought what an utter waste it was for this to have happened on Thanksgiving, when they might have slept until noon. Not that they ever would—or could—with Matthew and Bobby tiptoeing outside their door like elephants. But holidays and Sundays gave one a special feeling of latitude. She didn't have much feeling of any kind left at this point, and neither did David when he finally walked in, chilled, and tired, and full of frustration. Mary and Katie were already in the kitchen, and there was a smell of coffee rising. It didn't seem worth while to go back to bed. "Damn that pup," said David.

The sun came out later in the morning, and Claudia said, "Let's both escort him this time." They killed two birds with one stone and took Matthew with them while Bertha stayed with Bobby. They made an attractive family picture. There was nothing like a Great Dane to add éclat; Bluster had always dressed up the station wagon, too. "What a beautiful dog ! " people exclaimed as they strolled along the streets.

"All front and no back," Claudia muttered bitterly.

They walked and walked. "I bet we're going to the zoo," said Matthew, who by some odd process of reasoning was certain that this mass excursion into fresh air was for his especial benefit because Bobby was sick.

"Have another bet," said David.

"I bet we are going to the zoo ! " Matthew insisted knowingly.

"We have our own zooful," said Claudia.

He was considerably chagrined when they finally wound up at the familiar entrance of Beekman House, but nobody paid any attention to him because Bluster seemed to recognize the large tree in the courtyard. He stood by it thoughtfully for a moment before he lifted his leg to scratch his ear. David's breath exploded in the ultimate of despair. "Let's go home," he said wearily.

Claudia gave him a quick look. Was he really as tired as he sounded, or was he pretending this sudden exhaustion? She had noticed for the last block or two that his step had lost its spring, and now a thin white line of fatigue was etched faintly around his lips. She hoped, with a sinking of her heart, that he was not coming down with Bobby's grippe.

She didn't say anything about it, because he didn't like to be asked whether he felt well, particularly since the war. He was reluctant to admit any limitation of his physical well-being, and the intermittent attacks of malaria were a nagging reminder that his body was no longer the perfect organism that he had always thought of it as being. He was, in effect, much too good to get the grippe. "I'd rather be married to a hypochondriac," Claudia mumbled aloud.

"What?" he said.

"Nothing," she answered.

He seemed quite all right after they went upstairs, however, and got to talking business with John who was waiting for Candy to finish dressing.

"Any luck?" Candy asked, seeing Claudia through the mirror of her dressing-table.

Claudia shook her head.

"Oh for Heaven's sake," said Candy, "that silly dog. No matter what, though, John and I can take him out when we get back to-night. How do I look?"

"Fine," said Claudia. "You'd better hurry, it's almost one o'clock."

"There's time, dinner's not until two. Don't pick up the room, I know it's a mess—Katie said she'd do it—all those things on the chair need pressing—do you think I should have worn my blue suit instead of this dress?"

"No, you look lovely."

Candy twisted speculatively, appraising herself from several angles. "Personally, I think it's a little childish. I mean it could do more for my shape than it does. Claudia, if you saw me for the first time how old would you think I was?"

"Oh, about twenty-five or six."

"Liar. No, but really, look at me as if you were a stranger——"

Claudia rounded the thumb and first finger of each hand and put them against her eyes like spectacles. Candy giggled. "You're no help at all. Have I got too much lipstick on?"

"If you were five years older, you might have. Your waist-line's like a string bean. I hate you."

"Like fun you do. You wouldn't change places with anyone under the sun."

"You're right," said Claudia complacently.

David felt the same way about it. After Candy and John had gone, he said, "Funny, I have no desire to be that young again."

"That's good," said Claudia. "I haven't either. It wouldn't do us any good anyway," she added sensibly, "so we might as well grow old together gracefully."

"It's a deal," said David.

It started out to be a perfect Thanksgiving afternoon. Bobby, sneezing sloppily, but otherwise quite normal, was content to construct a plywood sailboat that John had brought him ; Matthew went to the park with Bertha, and David built a fire in the bedroom, with Shakespeare rubbing up against him, plastering strands of orange-coloured fur on his trousers. "I'll bat you one," he threatened, not really minding at all.

"This is like Sunday at the farm," said Claudia, as she turned back the spread.

"You miss the farm," said David.

"A little, yes. Don't you ? "

"Yes," said David.

Bluster liked the fire. He fell down in front of it, dropping each of his front paws separately. "That's for the benefit of the people downstairs," said Claudia. "Anyway, he seems happy and relaxed, so let us relax too and be happy."

"That's what I had in mind," said David.

He lay on the bed beside her and closed his eyes. She waited for a reasonable space, and then leaned on her elbow and looked down at him. "Hey," she protested, with indignation, "you're getting old a little too gracefully ! "

He seemed not to have heard her. He just lay there with the flickering light of the fire casting strange shadows on his face. "David——" she whispered in sudden terror.

He opened his eyes. "What's the matter ? "

"I didn't like your face."

"I'll get a new one."

"Don't bother, I'll try and fix the old one." She swung over to the floor. His hand was a rod of iron closing down on her arm. "Where are you going ? "

"None of your business."

"Come back here."

"Why ? You're not so interesting."

He was smart beyond belief, he must have seen the thermometer in her eye. " I will not take my temperature ! " he bellowed.

" Are you fighting ? " Bobby called out with interest from the other room.

" Your mother's found something else to worry about," David called back.

In the end, he held the thermometer between his lips, muttering, as he did so, that he was nothing but a henpeck. " Stop talking," she commanded, " or it won't register."

He looked at it before he gave it to her. " There, you little fool, it's absolutely normal."

She squinted at it professionally. " Ninety-nine and a half is not absolutely normal," she quibbled. Nevertheless she was enormously relieved, remembering that Bobby had begun with a hundred and three. She really was a fool ; naturally David was tired after not sleeping well for two nights in a row and being up at six this morning. " The trouble with you is," she said severely, striking while the iron was hot, " you're working too hard."

He flared up in earnest at that, and told her not to be any more of an idiot than she could help. Her feelings were hurt. She got off the bed, and scooped up the unsuspecting Shakespeare and installed herself in a chair with him to comb out his coat. After a little while, David got off the bed, too, and went into the bathroom, coming out again much too soon to have even a drink of water. She didn't realize what he was up to until he was smearing iodine on her scratches. " Now we're square for my temperature," he said with satisfaction.

The afternoon fairly flew after that. . . . Toward evening it started to rain, first in an intermittent spitting, and then in a heavy downpour. Bluster got as far as the front entrance, and reared back. " He never did like rain," Claudia recalled. " I'm glad."

" I'm glad you're glad," said David grimly.

" I didn't want you to get wet—would you mind very much taking your temperature just once more ? " she asked him, knowing perfectly well that she was overstepping the mark.

His hands reached for her neck. " Go ahead," she said meekly, " but it was a good try."

He hardly touched his supper. " How can I be hungry," he forestalled her, " when we had a big dinner and a late one ? "

"That's true," she acknowledged, and added in a burst of candour, "I don't know how you stand me."

"I don't either," he said.

She shifted her lips in humility. "I'm going to control this idiotic worrying," she promised him.

She expected him to meet her halfway, but instead he managed to elude her. "No sense in taking chances," he sheepishly confessed. "I think maybe I have got a little cold coming on."

Months, even years later, she could look back on that Thanksgiving evening and taste again the sense of utter desolation that had come over her. It was a thing apart from the quick, sharp anxiety she had felt for Bobby. She tried to fight it with all her strength and reason, but it got the better of her. "I suppose you wouldn't think of popping into bed with a hot lemonade," she suggested almost timidly.

"You suppose correctly," he replied.

It was ridiculous that she should have to handle him with kid gloves when it came to taking care of himself. She walked to the window, staring out into the fog on the river. Overhead, the lights of a plane blinked through the dark night. She followed it until it was out of sight. When she turned back into the room, David was settled in the corner of the sofa with a book, filling his pipe. It would be nice for both of them if she could settle herself with a book, too, but she knew she wouldn't be able to keep her mind on what she was reading. "I'm going to wash my hair," she decided restlessly.

Her head was in the basin for the last rinsing when David came in to tell her that Jerry Seymour was in the living-room. "He can't stay long, so hurry up."

"Oh, dear," said Claudia. "Why'd he come?"

"To see Candy. He didn't know she'd gone to Greenwich. She should have called him."

"She was going to call him tomorrow—is all the soap out?"

"Pretty much," he said. "Hurry up."

"Don't say 'pretty much.' Tell me where it isn't!"

"Isn't what?"

"Isn't out. The soap."

"Behind the ear, there's a little."

"Which ear?"

"Both. Why do you wash your hair anyway, at this hour of the night?"

"My nails needed it, I've been doing closets. Tell Jerry I'll be there in a minute."

He leaned across her to open the medicine chest, and she heard the rattle of the aspirin bottle. He must be feeling pretty miserable, she thought apprehensively, for he disdained medicine as a rule—not that he had any Christian Science leanings—it was simply a question of pride with him. As he walked out of the bathroom, he mentioned, in a kind of apology, "I've got a big day at the office tomorrow, I might as well check this thing."

"For once you're showing a little common-sense," she congratulated him. She wanted to say, "Over my dead body you're going to the office tomorrow," but some deep inner sanity kept her silent.

She dried her hair quickly, and slipped on a negligée that Julia had given her a long while ago. Jerry was the sort of man you wouldn't want to wear a woollen bathrobe in front of. He always tied a muffler around his neck when he wore a dressing-gown, which seemed to set him apart as a particular kind of person—not David's kind of person exactly—but no one was, as far as she was concerned, so it was nothing to hold against him.

He was talking about Elizabeth when she came into the living-room—telling David about the week they had spent in a little inn outside of London, and how they'd toured the countryside on bicycles. "I'd never have let her do it," he said, "if I had known. She seemed so well. It was so sudden. I keep blaming myself."

"Nonsense," David said. "There's nothing to blame yourself for. It was Elizabeth's time to go. And when the time comes it happens, and there's nothing we can do about it."

Claudia hated it when he went on like that. She was willing enough to adopt the philosophy in exclusive relation to her own time, but not David's or the children's. It meant that if they fell down the stairs, or choked to death on a piece of steak, or got shot by some lunatic, it would all be written off without so much as an excuse-me. It made one feel about as safe as walking through life on a tightrope. She changed the subject nervously. "Are you going to do a novel or another play next, Jerry?"

"I don't seem ready to begin anything quite yet," he said. "I don't know that I ever will. Self-expression doesn't seem as important to me as it used to. It's a sign of age, I suppose."

"It must be," she agreed lightly. "I feel the same way."

She observed him as he rose to leave. He really had aged since Elizabeth's death. Oldness had crept into the sag of his tall body, and his thick dark hair had turned white around the temples. He was finding it hard to make friends with pain. It was a phrase that her mother had once used, and suddenly it came into her mind.

"Tell Candy," he said, "that I wish she and young Payne would go out to dinner with me some evening before she goes back to college. I like him immensely."

"I didn't realize you knew him," said David. "Candy only met him after you and Elizabeth went to England."

"I know, but I remember him as a youngster. For years his family had a place at Edgartown. I used to visit an aunt of mine up there every summer."

"Isn't that odd, so did I," said Claudia. "Not every summer, though. I just went once."

And never again, she amended inwardly. People who didn't grow out of the Vineyard didn't really belong there. Certainly she hadn't belonged, and it was a month that had very nearly left her feeling inferior forever after. Everyone had been properly improper—even to their rudeness—while she'd been improperly proper. Everyone had been so healthy from sailing that they'd looked like handsome buttons on a card, making her feel spindly against their bronzed magnificence. It was something of a shock to realize that John's younger self had been at home in one of those pretentiously modest little houses that used the sea for lawn instead of grass and flowers. She wondered whether John's mother was of the same soft hardness that she remembered her aunt to have been. Scratch her large, motherly bosom and you didn't get bosom, you just got breeding. How would it work out with Candy, who had been raised from a tradition of rolling fields, and warm and living impulses?

"I hope it's been a successful family dinner for her," she said, following her thoughts. "I hope they like her."

"They can't help but like her," said Jerry. "She's Elizabeth's daughter." He held out his hand. "Good night. And let me come up again sometime soon."

"You don't need an invitation."

"But you always seem so happy and complete in yourselves."

"We are," said Claudia, "and it's not good, I suppose."

"It's the best thing in life," said Jerry. "It's worth the whole price of admission."

David looked as if he were about to add something, and then thought better of it. He knocked his pipe out against the ash tray. " I might as well go down with you. I have to take the dog out again."

Claudia threw discretion to the winds. " David, please, you just took aspirin. It's foolish to go out into the cold. It's raining, besides. Let him wait until Candy and John come."

He eyed Bluster speculatively. " I wouldn't dare," he said. " It might be the straw that broke the camel's back—or, in this case, its physical equivalent."

" I'll take him," Jerry offered. " Come along, Bluster, old boy, will you go with me ? "

Claudia was surprised at his offering. She'd always had a suspicion that Jerry's respect of Bluster's size and weight verged a little upon timidity. She accepted with alacrity before he changed his mind.

" That was a dirty trick," David remarked as the door closed upon them.

" He said he'd like to," she defended lamely.

" But he didn't know that Bluster goes out just to admire the scenery. The poor devil will be standing half the night, waiting for that fool pup."

Scarcely five minutes later they heard the clang of the elevator. They rushed to find out what it was all about. Jerry tossed the leash to them and gave Bluster an affectionate little shove. " Go along, old fellow, that was very nice, we'll do it again, sometime." He waved and stepped back into the waiting elevator. The door slid to, and he was gone.

At last Claudia found her voice. " Do what again ? "

" Ask Bluster," said David.

They asked Bluster, but he wouldn't talk. However, he was very thirsty, and sloshed up gallons of water.

They talked about Jerry while they undressed.

" My heart ached for him," said Claudia. " It must have been such a lonely Thanksgiving. He hasn't anything to be thankful for."

" I think he has," said David. " Jerry had more happiness in the few months with Elizabeth than most people have in a lifetime. It doesn't make any difference how long, it's how much."

" I'd want it long, too." She shivered suddenly.

" Is the window open too much ? " David asked.

" A little."

She let him close it halfway, but she knew that it wasn't

the chill air from the river that had made her cold. " Hop into bed, quick," she said. " And remind me to have Jerry over for dinner soon. It wouldn't have hurt me to ask him today. People who are awfully happy get awfully self-centred. Like a horse with blinkers."

" Move over, horse," he said. " It's not a very brilliant simile," he added.

" I'm not supposed to be brilliant," she said. " I'm just supposed to be attractive."

They were asleep in no time. It might have been minutes or hours later that David awakened in a fit of coughing. He couldn't seem to stop, and as he struggled against the paroxysm, he became furious and apologetic at the same time. " I'm sorry, darling, some lint from the blankets must have gotten into my throat."

It didn't sound as if it were lint from the blankets. She rose and closed the window.

" What are you doing that for ? "

" Sit up a little. Maybe that'll help."

It didn't help. Coughing that didn't stop was the most horrible sound in the world. The room was freezing, but her gown clung damply to her skin. She was glad he could not see the way her heart was pounding. " I'll get you some water," she said.

" I'll get it."

" You'll do nothing of the kind. Stay quiet."

The water didn't help either. " Damn——" he muttered.

" Don't try to talk. I'll heat some milk and honey. That's Bertha's remedy."

She hurried to the kitchen. Candy's door stood ajar ; a shaft of light from the window fell across the empty bed. Claudia glanced at her watch. It was after one o'clock. " That child ought to be home," she registered vaguely, but the rasp of David's coughing blocked out all other thoughts. Even Bobby didn't matter ; she passed his room without pausing to glance in at him.

She put the milk on to boil and hoped that they weren't out of honey. Mary came into the kitchen while she was looking for it, a different person in her plaid blanket robe and long Irish hair. " Is the boy bad again ? " she enquired in quick solicitude.

" No, it's Mr. David this time."

" Oh dear, he's after taking Bobby's cold," Mary exclaimed. " They're that catching. My cousin's whole family, the whole eight of them, came down sick last winter, and Georgie, the oldest, went into pneumonia."

" Did he get all right ? "

Mary looked embarrassed, and Claudia could tell that she was sorry she had brought the matter up. Georgie had very likely died.

David wasn't coughing when she returned with the hot milk. " See how much good it's done you already," she said flippantly, to cover her relief. She didn't like the way he looked, though. There was an air of exhaustion about him and a bright spot of colour on either cheek. He made a fuss about drinking the milk—wouldn't even touch it until it had completely cooled off—so she knew there would be no use asking him to take his temperature. " You wouldn't let me call Dr. Mack ? " she suggested timidly.

" I would not," he replied with finality.

She sank to the edge of the bed, numb with anxiety, and mute with the helplessness of not being able to do anything for him. He seemed to take pity on her. " You poor little old slob," he said. " For a lady in a delicate condition you certainly have your hands full, also."

" Woman's work is never done," she managed to joke.

" I suppose you're aching to get that thermometer in my mouth."

" How'd you know it ? "

" Oh, all right," he gave in magnanimously, " let's have it."

He rolled his eyes and made foolish faces while he held the stick between his lips. She tried to smile along with him. It wasn't natural for her knees to be shaking like this. It must be her delicate condition after all.

He took the thermometer out of his mouth and looked at it. " Perfectly normal," he assured her and shook it down before he gave it to her. " There," he said, " I hope you're satisfied."

She was anything but satisfied, but his gesture tied her hands neatly and effectively. His fever must have been pretty high, if he didn't want her to see it. She dreaded the morning. How was she going to keep him from going to the office ? He was too good to be like Mary's Georgie, he was a law unto himself, not heir to human illness or disease. She remembered a bad cold that he had had the first few months they were married. He had bought Shakespeare to take her mind off him while he got over it in peace.

" This is the time a double bed is a nuisance," he broke into her thoughts. " I'll sleep on the couch, so you don't catch this bug that seems to be going around."

" Don't be ridiculous. If there's any sleeping on couches to be done I'll do it. Only I have no intention of budging from here."

" I might keep you awake."

" You won't."

" You might keep me awake."

" Have I ever ? "

Candy and John came home while they were arguing about it. They looked as if they had stepped out of Heaven, and the fact that the household was up at that hour was part of the especial functioning of their universe. They didn't notice the hot milk, or the thermometer on the night-table, or anything else. " Surprise ! " they cried in a single voice.

" You're engaged," said Claudia mechanically, with her mind on David.

Candy's face fell in disappointment. " Who told you ! "

" We can't find anyone to surprise," John rebelled.

" Never mind, darling," Candy placated him. " I'm going to call Jerry in the morning, and he'll be surprised."

David laughed. It was funny enough to laugh about, but instead the tears began to stream down Claudia's cheeks. Suddenly Candy began to cry too. " It's from happiness," she gulped.

It was a strange moment in the night, full of darkness and stars.

SIX

THE WINTER started off with everybody coughing, and people bragging that they had or hadn't caught the flu. David bragged the loudest of all, because he said he'd refused to give in to an attack of it, and had gone down to the office the next morning and worked it off. "Very smart," Claudia upbraided him bitterly when she heard him say it the first time. "Only you didn't work it off, you're still coughing."

"So is half of New York."

"You wouldn't be, if you'd listened to me and stayed in bed like any sensible human being."

"If I'd listened to you, I'd have been laid up for weeks."

He got his comeuppance, bragging so much, when Edith Dexter asked him at one of Julia's dinner parties, whether he had gone into Science. She said it in capital letters, which was a clue that she had herself been a Christian Scientist before she'd given it up in favour of glandular injections. No one was supposed to know about the injections, although everyone did, and everyone said that they must be wearing off, because Edith was getting old under the neck, and showed bags and puffs in a strong light. Having looked so abruptly and startlingly youthful for upward of a year, the change was a trifle shocking, yet really all she was doing was paying up on borrowed time.

Her interest in David's metaphysical development made Claudia feel that Edith wasn't too far from reverting to Science again. Ever since her son's death, years ago, she'd been going from one thing to another. It was Edith, as a matter of fact, who had first started Julia off on spiritualism. "That was a first-rate bunch of second-rate mentalities," David commented sourly as they drove home in a taxi that evening. He was still disgruntled from having been taken for a Christian Scientist, and Claudia had no sympathy for him. "Blame yourself," she said shortly. "You sound the image of one, and I'm not at all certain that deep down inside that so-called tough-minded mind of yours, you haven't got leanings in that direction."

He snorted.

"Go ahead and snort," she said. "If it isn't so, why won't you let Dr. Mack go over you?"

"Firstly, I'd have to be half dead before I let that pompous little monkey come near me, and secondly, there's nothing wrong with me ; I never felt better."

"That's what I mean," said Claudia, "listen to yourself."

"Look," he demanded, sounding more like one every minute, "do you want to wish something on me ? "

Her heart turned over. "That's a dreadful thing to say."

"Well, you'll do it," he insisted cruelly.

"Do you actually think thinking has power ? " she asked in a small voice.

"I actually do," he said.

She could see that he was teasing, but even so, the idea was a profoundly disturbing one. She sat huddled in the corner of the cab, full of conflict. He took pity on her. "Don't be a little ass," he said.

"You shouldn't have said it."

"That you're a little ass ? But you are."

"No, the other thing. About wishing something on you."

"Then turn over a new leaf."

"I'll try to," she said meekly.

"That's a good girl." He leaned forward. "Go around the park a couple of times," he told the driver.

"But he can't, we're almost to Beekman Place ! "

"There's no law about changing one's course."

"If you're trying to sound symbolic," she said, "I'm not impressed. Anyway, this is a fine waste of money. It's miles out of our way."

He put his arm around her. "What's the matter, you used to ride around the park with me."

"That was when you were single." She pulled away. "Encouraging a married man is different."

"Whimsey, whimsey," he chided.

"Besides, this is no weather for pleasure driving. It's freezing ; there's no heat in this cab."

"According to Julia's hysterical conversation with me at the dinner table this evening we'd better get used to freezing."

"But you told me that the coldest thing about Iceland was its name. You said it isn't much worse than our climate here."

"It was Julia's fine-feathered friends in the next world who said it was cold," he reminded her. "Have you forgotten that they've promised us we're going to a cold climate ? "

"No, I haven't forgotten, and you haven't either, apparently," she retorted. "For all your snorting, you're a lot more susceptible than you let on."

" Don't be another ass," he said. " And don't mess up the
ride with being nasty or I'll dump you out in the street and
let you walk home."

" You're ruining my hair."

" What of it ? "

" I want to use it again tomorrow. It cost three dollars,
Julia made me have it set at her man's. I could kick myself
for listening to her. And I could kick myself for letting her
talk me into having this dress made, too. ' You have to spend
a little money on yourself if you live in New York. Remember
you're the wife of a successful architect ! ' "

" Well, aren't you ? "

" Yes, just look at me. You're successful in everything you
do. That's exactly the point, I can't wear the blasted dress
much longer—I suppose everybody could tell, couldn't they ? "

" Not at all."

She was partially diverted, even though she suspected he
was lying. " I didn't show with Bobby and Matthew, either,
remember ? "

" I remember." He laughed. " Come over here."

Before she knew it, she had limbered up against him
" Careful," he said, and rescued from his breast pocket one c‑
the big black cigars that Hartley had handed out at dinner.

" You don't look well in a cigar anyway," she said. " You
ought to discipline yourself to two pipes a day. You look
nice in pipes, and they make you smell much better."

" There's nothing wrong with the smell from one of
Hartley's cigars." He bit off the end and put it in his mouth
with his free hand. " Excuse my other arm a moment," he
said.

He lit the cigar, and coughed as he drew on it. She must
have tensed without realizing it, because he apologized
elaborately for swallowing the wrong way.

" Don't pass it off as a joke," she said. " You always find
an excuse. What made you cough on and off all evening ?
Were you swallowing wrong the whole time ? "

" Oh Lord," he said, " here we are, right back where we
started from."

" I can't help it, you make me so mad ! "

" Where's that new leaf you were going to turn over ? "

" I don't see why I should, when you're so unreasonable.
So damn pigheaded ! "

" The driver will think we're quarrelling," he said mildly.

" We are ! If you must know it, Philip Dexter told me

tonight that you look like you'd lost a lot of weight, and it worried me to death."

"Philip Dexter's jealous. He's getting paunchy."

"Then you have lost ? "

"I have not."

"How do you know, did you weigh yourself ? "

"What for ? "

She bit her lips to keep from crying with frustration, and then all at once, he began to humour her, because she was pregnant, probably. "I'll tell you what I'll do," he said magnanimously, "I'll hop on the scale when we get home."

"And take your temperature too," she threw in for good measure.

"I haven't got a temperature ! " he bellowed.

"Shh ! The driver will think we're quarrelling. How do I know you haven't ? Sometimes I feel you in bed, and you're very warm."

"Would you rather I was very cool ? "

"You know perfectly well what I mean." She sat forward. "Driver, turn around please, we're going back."

Bluster met them in the hall, wagging his tail in gigantic arcs of welcome, and Shakespeare meandered out too, pretending indifference, but really very glad to see them. "This is as good as being on the farm," said Claudia. "Better, even. You don't have to go down to the cellar to shake the furnace."

"No, but I have to go down to the street to shake the dog," said David.

There was a special delivery letter from Candy. Claudia read it while she was waiting for him to come back. Candy wrote in a half-print that gave the appearance of being easy to read, but wasn't. It took some little while to decipher that college was a ghastly bore and a beastly waste of time (or vice versa, it didn't make much difference) and Candy was beginning to wonder what was the sense of it all, and would Claudia be an angel and put the enclosed card in some roses —expensive ones with long stems—and send them to John's mother for her birthday next Saturday ? The card read, "To Mother Payne, with love from your new daughter, Candy."

"From the general feel of this letter," David remarked when he read it, "Candy's not going to wait until she graduates to get married."

"That's two years from now—I wouldn't either."

"You didn't even finish high school."

"Don't make me out so ignorant, I was in my first year

at the Dramatic Academy when you came along. Hurry up
and get undressed. And don't flatter yourself—I only want
you to get weighed."

"You've got a one-track mind like nobody's business. I'll
do it in the morning."

"I don't trust you in the morning. You'll do it now."

He might just as well not have got on the scales for all the
satisfaction it gave her. He teetered back and forth until his
weight veered from a hundred and seventy-three to a hundred
and ninety-six, which was ridiculous, for he had never weighed
as much as a hundred and ninety-six in his life, nor as little as
a hundred and seventy-three. "You clown," she scolded.
"Stand still ! "

"These silly bathroom scales aren't any good, anyway," he
said. "Come on to bed."

"Not until you take your temperature."

"Look——" he began.

"Shut up," she said. "You promised."

She made him keep the thermometer between his lips for
a full minute and a half, and then got hold of it before he
could shake it down. "Ninety-nine and two-tenths," she read.

"Absolutely normal. Now will you let me alone ? "

"Ninety-eight six is normal."

"You're psychotic. You've got to get over this senseless
worrying."

"I've never worried without reason."

"You worried about Bobby ; you magnified a little cold
into all sorts of things."

"He had a hundred and four, I was entitled to worry."

"Well, I've only got ninety-nine."

"Ninety-nine two."

"Claudia, listen to me." He drew her down beside him on
the bed. "I'm in dead earnest, you'll have to turn over that
new leaf we were talking about. You owe it to me and to
yourself and to the baby. You simply have to begin to take
things easy."

"I couldn't have things any easier than I have, with Mary
and Katie."

"I'm talking about your mind."

"I get feelings," she mumbled.

"I know you do, and it's hell on all of us."

"If only you wouldn't work so hard. You haven't been
home once this week before half-past seven. And then you're
so tired you can hardly eat."

"I eat plenty, and you only imagine I'm tired."

"I don't imagine it."

"All right, I'm tired," he said, "and I'm working hard. What of it? I've waited a long time to get back in the saddle again. After a couple of years in the jungle, and months of inactivity on the farm, it's a great and glorious feeling to be functioning again. Don't nag me to live frugally, just so that you shouldn't worry about me. I'm serious, Claudia. It isn't fair."

"I suppose it isn't," she agreed unhappily.

She lay awake for a long while, mulling over everything that he had said, examining her secret self. Was it true that she was nagging him to take care of himself because her inner security was dependent upon his physical well-being? She didn't like to admit it, she would rather believe that this strange anxiety was a symptom of her pregnancy—the way some women flew into tantrums or wanted pickles. Whichever way it was, though, he was right. It was not fair to make him a victim of her fears.

He coughed a little. She made herself lie perfectly still, so that he would think she was asleep, and hadn't heard him.

The talk must have done David good, too, because he was home at half-past six the next evening. Claudia didn't fool herself, he was probably a new broom sweeping clean, but at least she had made a little headway with him.

They were almost embarrassed with the extra time on their hands. He said "hello" to the boys, who had just sat down to their cereal, and asked the dog if he was a good dog, and then washed up, and looked at his watch. "What time is dinner?" he asked pointedly.

She had tried to hurry it as soon as she'd heard his key in the latch, but it was a loin of pork and it couldn't be hurried. "Quarter to eight," she said.

He looked at his watch again, as much as to say what good did it do him to come home early when he had to wait an eternity for his dinner? "Darling, we're not mind readers," she informed him with unction. "We didn't expect you an hour ahead of time, but if you're hungry, we can switch to eggs."

"I'm not hungry," he said, distantly.

He sat down in a straight chair, like a stranger in the house, meting out a silent punishment with the very way he sat there, not even reading the paper. Claudia stood it as long as she could.   Then she announced, very quietly, " Watch out, I'm going to scream," and opened her mouth and did so.   The children came running.   "What's the matter ? " they demanded in a single breath.

" Mamma screamed," said David blandly.   Then everybody laughed, and David roughhoused with Bluster until the chandeliers shook, and Shakespeare darted under the armchair for safety, and when dinner was finally announced, it had to be kept warm in the oven because David was in the middle of a draughts game with Bobby.

After dinner, he made himself comfortable on the sofa with a paper-bound detective story, and Claudia tacked up the hem of the dress she had worn the night before.   They didn't even have to talk.   " See ? " she said, contentedly.

" Um," said David.

The jangle of the telephone was a violation of the peace that filled the room.   " I'll go," said David, without moving.

" No, I'll go," said Claudia.

Neither of them moved.   Mary came to the door.   " I thought you were out," she said, " until I saw the light in here. It's Mrs. Dexter on the line."

" For me or Mr. Naughton ? "

" She asked for you."

" What should she want to talk to me for ? " David injected with a scowl.

" I thought maybe she wanted you to go to church with her next Wednesday night," said Claudia demurely.

" Humph," he said.

" All you can say is Humph and Um."

She came back in a little while and went on with her sewing.

" What'd she want ? " David eventually weakened.

" Who ? "

" You know who."

" Edith ? "

" Jump in the lake," he said.

" Whoever says men aren't as curious as women is crazy," said Claudia.   " I've tested you out time and again."

" I don't care, don't tell me," he said.

She rose and kissed him, ruffling his hair, which he detested. " You're so cute," she said.

" Hey, stop it."   By a swift and almost painless manipulation of her arm, he pulled her down on his lap and bit the tip of her ear.   She slapped his face.   " Don't do that, it drives me crazy ! "

3

" It drives me crazy," he mimicked in a high falsetto, and did it again.

A short while later they went to bed. " Edith really did want us for next Wednesday. She's having a dinner party," Claudie remembered at the last minute.

" No thanks," said David.

" That's what I told her. They're going to the opening of Jim Varney's play afterwards."

" Oh," said David, " I thought you wanted to see it."

" I do. We'll go sometime, if it runs long enough."

" Why don't you want to go to the opening ? Jim's been so decent to you, it wouldn't hurt you to be there."

" I'm sure we can't get tickets at this late date."

" Then go with Edith."

" Without you ? Since when."

" I didn't say ' without me,' I'd like to go."

She eyed him with suspicion. " What lies behind this sudden rush of nobility ? "

" I've been doing a lot of thinking this evening," he said slowly. " I think we ought to stop leading a hermit's existence."

" Are you bored with me ? Wasn't it a nice evening ? "

" It was a lovely evening," he said. " But not good for what ails us. We ought to get out more."

" When two people love each other and are content to be alone together," Claudia maintained, " it's worth the whole price of admission. That was a very apt expression of Jerry's."

" But he forgot to tell you about the deferred payment that usually comes when the picnic's over," David said.

" This picnic isn't ever going to be over."

" It's got to be. Everything comes to an end."

Because she knew so well what he meant, she quickly changed the subject—in the same cowardly fashion she always shied away from any mention of life insurance or wills, or trust funds. " You've fixed it so that I have to lead a hermit's existence," she said.

" Nonsense. The baby won't be here until April. You've got the whole winter ahead of you to have a good time in."

" What kind of a good time ? "

" Meet people. Have people in."

" You sound like Julia."

" Julia's right for once. I'm glad she made you get some nice clothes."

" What good are they ? "

" They must have seams to let out."

" They wouldn't be fit to wear afterwards."

" Then get some new ones."

" For a few months ? I wouldn't dream of it."

" Well, what do other women do ? " he said impatiently.
" They seem to manage to go around fully clothed."

He had her cornered. " Why all this business about building
up a social life all of a sudden ? " she demanded.
" Especially at a time when you're working your head off ? "

" Ha," he said. " I thought that was it."

" Of course it's it. You forget that the first thing you said
when I told you about Edith was ' No thanks.' "

" I had no right to say it. Why don't you kick my tail and
remind me that you're entitled to a little fun and excitement
occasionally ? "

" It doesn't mean anything to me."

" It should."

" Well, I'm sorry. It doesn't, and that's that."

" It's not normal, this sticking home every night."

" Then I'm not normal. And anyway, we don't stick home
every night. We go to the movies, and take walks, and long
drives——"

" But always together. By ourselves."

" Yes. And I wouldn't want it any different, no matter
what the final payment."

He lit his last cigarette before turning the light out. " Did
it ever occur to you," he said, " that I might like a little
diversion myself once in a while ? "

" But you said, ' No thank you,' " she persisted obstinately.

" All right, I was shortsighted. Edith is no great shakes,
but that doesn't mean we mightn't meet some interesting
people at her house. Call her up first thing in the morning,
and tell her that we'll come."

" She's probably asked someone else already."

David's lips went sideways in a crooked grin. " She'll
manage to have us," he said.

She glanced at him out of the corner of her eye. Edith
undoubtedly would manage. He was more than attractive,
standing there in his pyjamas—put together with bone and
muscle, without an ounce of flabbiness inside or out. Any
woman would be crazy about him, and although she was
certain that he was putting on this show entirely for her sake,
he might surprise himself by having a nice time if they did go
out a little. It might be good for his general health, too. Two

things couldn't occupy the same space at the same time, and if he had to go out to dinner, he'd have to come home early to dress, and if he stayed up late, he'd sleep longer in the morning. "Fine!" she said. "I'd love to go to Edith's, but I didn't want to say so. Opening nights are fun."

It was his turn to glance at her out of the corner of his eye. "Fine!" he echoed.

They'd got themselves into a fine mess, she reflected gloomily.

SEVEN

EDITH WAS ASLEEP when Claudia called up the next morning.
It was hard to remember that most women didn't get up
early. She supposed that Edith didn't have anything to get
up early for.

At noon Edith called back. Her face fell over the phone,
and Claudia knew at once that she must have asked someone
else in their place, but she gave no indication that she had.
"Claudia dear, I couldn't be happier," she exclaimed.
"David's such a wonderful person, I've always felt a strange
sense of attunement with him. And of course," she added
generously, "Phil was devoted to you that winter you spent
in New York, so it's really very nice discovering each other
again after all these years."

"Awfully nice," Claudia agreed, wondering how Edith was
going to get hold of two extra seats at the last moment.

"Seven o'clock dinner, sharp," said Edith.

It showed how countrified they were, because they got there
at seven o'clock sharp. They were not only the first to arrive,
but Edith and Phil were nowhere in sight. The butler helped
them off with their wraps, trying to look as if he hadn't been
interrupted in the middle of the salad dressing, and said that
Mr. and Mrs. Dexter would be with them immediately.

"Immediately" turned out to be a good fifteen minutes,
during which David complained bitterly for having broken
not only his neck but his last appointment to get there on
time, and Claudia said it served him right, whose idea was it
to come in the first place ? He cheered up, however, when
the butler appeared with a shaker of cocktails and a tray of
canapés, and left them on the coffee table, presumably to keep
them happy and occupied. "Are the cocktails good ? "
Claudia asked in an undertone.

"Fair," said David.

"Have a canapé."

"Are they good ? "

"I don't think so. They seem to be made on crackers
instead of toast." She selected one, hoping that it was paté,
but it was peanut butter. "This is the crowning indignity,"
she said. "What time is it ? "

" We won't get to the theatre before the curtain goes up, if that's what you've got in mind," said David.

" It's what I had in mind," said Claudia. " Why doesn't Edith do something about this room I wonder ? It's got too much of everything in it, including oriental rugs and bric-a-brac."

" It all belonged in the big house that her mother had," said David.

" Who told you ? "

" I just know," said David. " It reeks of it. Those are pretty fine Chelsea pieces on the mantel, I wouldn't mind owning them."

" I would. They look like birthday cake."

" You just don't like Chelsea."

" Odd, because I like cake. I think it's on account of her son dying."

" What is ? "

" That Edith doesn't take an interest in her home."

Before David could answer, Phil hurried in with the distracted air of having tied his tie on the way down the hall, and a few moments later Edith appeared in green taffeta that rustled, and too much rouge on one cheek. She shook hands with Claudia, and almost kissed David. She did not seem at all disturbed at the lateness of the hour, so Claudia said, " I do hope we won't miss the first act."

Edith looked at her vaguely, and said, " Pinky's late as usual." Her thin eager hand lighted for an instant on David's knee. " You know Pinky, Pinky Farnham ? "

" No," said David.

" Pinky Farnham " sounded, thought Claudia, as if she might be quite young and pretty, but Pinky turned out to be a bald-headed little man, with more charm than he should have had, and a rich voice that was deep without being masculine. He escorted a sprightly lady who wore a moustache on her upper lip, and twitched. Claudia tried not to look at either the moustache or the twitch on account of the baby, but it was hard to keep from it. " I didn't catch her name," she said to Phil in an undertone.

" Why, that's Minerva Train," he told her, as if he were surprised that she didn't know.

" What does she do ? "

" Writes a column, lectures, and runs for things."

" Is she married ? "

" Good God, no ! " said Phil.

"I didn't see how she could be," said Claudia.

Phil looked at her, and all of a sudden he gave a laugh that made him sound like David. They might have revived their old interest in each other if they could have sat together at the table, but Edith had arranged it differently. She gave Phil to Minerva, and David to herself, and Pinky to Claudia. Pinky looked bored around the eyebrows, but to be quite fair to him, it was no great stimulation to sit next to a woman who was pregnant. "You don't have to talk to me," Claudia assured him affably. "I'm quite happy just eating."

"I say," he said, although he wasn't English. After a moment he remarked thoughtfully, "I don't think it's enough to make you happy. I mean to say, Edith keeps an expensive cook, but her dinners are utterly foul."

He was rude but right. The soup was black bean, dressed up with hard-boiled egg and a slice of lemon, but Claudia recognized that it was out of a can because she did the same trick herself upon occasion. "I loathe beans," Pinky went on in growing indignation. "Beans in any shape or form."

"Shhh," Claudia whispered. "Edith'll hear you."

"I want her to hear me," Pinky said. "Edith knows how I feel about her food, don't you darling?" he called across the table in his melodious voice.

"What, darling?" Edith paused to tear her eyes from David's face.

"Nothing, darling," said Pinky. "Eat your nice din-din."

It was now clear that Pinky made a career of being incorrigible. Dullness settled like a heavy mist upon Claudia's spirit, for she knew that she was going to trail behind his sparkling repartee in spurts of heavy ineptness. Perfected competence in any one department of conduct always affected her adversely. She had already gathered that Pinky spent the major part of his time visiting important people from Bar Harbour to Palm Beach, according to season, which meant that he probably packed his glittering little phrases in his suitcase and used them in one place after another, until even "din-din" shone with polished brilliance.

She couldn't imagine David saying "din-din," or having such felicity for rudeness. Next to Pinky, they were both mere diamonds in the rough.

"I do wish," she followed up aloud, "that nobody would bother with coffee."

Pinky's voice threw up its hands in a tiny shriek. "What a

ghastly idea ! " he protested. " Personally I shan't budge without it, and that's final."

" But we'll miss part of the first act if we don't hurry."

" My dear girl, I haven't seen a first act in years. After all, why should one ? "

" Now you're just being an ass," said Claudia shortly.

Pinky bestowed a beaming smile upon her. " You're very sweet," he said. " Really very sweet."

She ignored the blandishment. " The least you could do," she insisted, " is to be on time, especially since you're all friends of Jim Varney's."

" Poor old Jim," said Pinky comfortably, " he's been having one flop after another, hasn't he ? "

" All the more reason."

" Sheer sophistry." Pinky nibbled a piece of forgotten celery, being as cunning as a rabbit about it. " Darling, you should have seen that putrid little number of Jerry Seymour's he did last spring. *Happy Trouble* it was called. Fancy that."

" I did fancy it, and it wasn't putrid," Claudia denied hotly. " It started out by being called *Sad Ecstasy*, and it was a quite good play until the producer decided to turn it into a farce."

" Author's alibi," said Pinky.

" In this case it's true. I happen to know, because I was in it."

Pinky scrutinized her in mild astonishment. " Dearie me," he said, " I didn't know you were an actress, why doesn't somebody tell me these things ? "

" I wasn't for very long, and I'm not any more."

" Weren't you any good at it ? "

" I was very good at it. Jim offered me a job in his next play."

" Oh,"—Pinky glanced across at David, who was listening to Minerva hold forth on labour unions—" I see," he said.

" You see what ? "

" Husband preferred wife to be homebody."

" On the contrary. David was all for it."

" I see," said Pinky again, " then you'll probably go back on the stage "—he cleared his throat delicately—" afterwards."

She was a little disgruntled. " I didn't think it was that obvious," she said. " Anyway, you're not in the least interested in either my domestic life or my career."

" Quite true," he admitted with engaging candour. " I was just making a pretty bit of chit-chat. Let's talk about French prints now, shall we? I bid in a divine Janninet at the Von Steinmetz sale last week for less than half its valuation. The dealers must have been asleep. There are two kinds of people, don't you think? Those who adore French prints and those who don't."

"I'm the other kind," said Claudia. "Please pass the almonds."

"They're soggy," said Pinky, "have a peppermint. Your husband's a banker, isn't he?"

"No, David's brother Hartley is the banker."

"Oh yes, what am I thinking of? The bean soup must have gone to my head, instead. Julia's your sister-in-law, of course! Dear old Julia, I met her at a séance last week. A new medium just came over from England, and the Fitzhughs were trying him out with a selected group. Awful fake—trumpet and all that. Julia has a good medium, I hear, but she's not telling. Try and get the name for me, will you? What did you say your husband is?"

"He's a dentist," said Claudia.

It was good for the baby to see the nonplussed look on Pinky's face. Her self-confidence returned. With a little practice she could probably learn the art of subtle discourtesy, and become a social success.

They arrived at the theatre in time for the first intermission. "I knew we wouldn't be late," said Pinky, as he scanned the audience for familiar faces. They both caught sight of Helen Drew at the same moment. It would have been hard to miss her, for she looked like a resplendent rooster, with her head full of feathers, and green gloves rippling all the way up to her shoulders. "Claudia darling!" she exclaimed in a brand new throaty voice, "how grand to see you! And Pinky, Angel!"

"Helen, my pet!" cried Pinky.

Helen-my-Pet and Pinky-Angel fell into each other's arms, only to be torn apart by the milling crowds making for the lobby. "Darlings, dinner next Monday night at eight!" Helen called after them feverishly. "I'll phone you both tomorrow!"

"Adore it!" Pinky called back. "That dreadful woman," he remarked to Claudia. "How do you happen to know her?"

"We went to school together. Was the nice old man she was with her father, I wonder?"

" Firstly," Pinky elucidated, " he is not a nice old man. He is a very un-nice old man with scads of money. Secondly, Helen never had a father. They just lifted up a stone, and there she was."

" I don't think that's very funny," said Claudia.

" Everybody else does," said Pinky. " I've been saying it for years. There's Julia. The old girl is getting scrawny, by Gad."

" Where ?   I don't see her."

" Over by the door. She must have gone to the Satterlees for dinner ; I was there last night. Top drawer, but grisly bores. Come on, let's see who else is with them."

Claudia didn't know any of Julia's group, although one of the women looked familiar. " Claudia, you know Madame Beritza——? " Julia's voice was like a well-bred nudge. " Carra, don't you remember my little sister-in-law ?   We stopped off at her farm a few years ago when we were driving up to Boston to one of your concerts."

" But of course, of course, of course ! "

Claudia recalled that Beritza always said everything three times, which was about the only thing that was the same about her, for her black hair was a brilliant yellow and her teeth were stunning. " I have only just got back today from Hollywood ! " she carolled on, at the top of her famous voice. " And I must see all my friends right away quick, so tomorrow you will come along to cocktails at my hotel, no ? "   She caught Pinky's hand in both of hers. " And the sweet little husband, how well I remember him, he must surely come too."

" Without the shadow of a doubt," Pinky solemnly accepted, " the sweet little husband will be there."

" Would you believe," he demanded, as Beritza was swept away from them, " that we've never actually met ?   Beritza and I ? "

" I'd believe anything," said Claudia coldly.

He was impervious to the barb. " No, but truly," he rambled on, " either I was in Paris, and she was in London, or she was in New York and I was somewhere else——"

Claudia wasn't listening to him. She had caught sight of David, standing out on the sidewalk talking to Phil in the freezing wind. " Excuse me," she broke in, and left Pinky gesticulating to thin air.

She had almost managed to push through to the outer doors, when Jim Varney scuttled in from the backstage entrance, and bumped into her. He literally clapped his hand over her

mouth. "Let me get out of here," he muttered, and grabbed
her by the arm and pulled her after him into the box office.
There were two men and a woman and an electric stove in
the cubicle, which made it almost as crowded as the
lobby.

"What the hell do you think you're doing, Varney ! " one
of the men objected, " you can't bring anybody in here who
isn't bonded ! "

"Don't be a horse's neck, Max, this kid's a friend
of mine ! Look baby——" Jim fixed her with feverish
eyes. "What are they saying out there, did it go over, do
they like it ? "

It occurred to her, belatedly, that no one had even
bothered to mention the play. "They seem to be liking it,"
she faltered.

"You lie," said Jim. "These goddamn opening nights are
murder, and by God, I'm going to take steps to do away with
them——"

"Go ahead and try it," said Max, "and see how far it gets
you."

The woman snapped a rubber band around a stack of tickets
and yawned as she reached for her hat and coat. "I'm going
home," she said. "Ta, ta, see you tomorrow." She paused
at the door. "I hope there's a big long line waiting for me
in the morning," she said, "but my personal opinion is that
we fell on our face. There was a terrible lot of coughing
during the first act, and you know what that means."

"It doesn't mean anything because everyone has colds,"
said Claudia, and realized it anew with relief. True, David
had coughed a little on and off all evening, but so, according
to the box office, had the rest of the audience.

"Having a nice time ? " he whispered to her on the way
back to their seats.

"I am, now," she said.

"Phil's got a reservation at some night club. I told him
we'd go."

It turned out to be three night clubs, but like the White
Queen, they always found the same people sitting at the table
next to them, so everyone might just as well have stayed in
one place to begin with. At two o'clock, Jim wandered in
with the morning papers under his arm. He was quite drunk
and indiscriminately affectionate, for all the reviews were raves
except one, and that one was a rave, because the reviewer
loathed it. Suddenly everybody began to talk about the play.

They said how wonderful it was, which was just the opposite of what they had said before they'd found out it was a hit.

"Human nature is peculiar," Claudia said to David as they rolled into bed a little before dawn.

"Very peculiar." He put his arm around her.

"It's so frightfully late," she murmured.

"It hardly pays to go to sleep," he said.

When Candy came home for the Christmas holidays, she couldn't get over how social they had become. She sat on the bed, watching Claudia dress for Beritza's come-back concert. Claudia wasn't crazy about a whole evening of singing, but Julia said she'd bought four boxes, and somebody had to use them.

"How did all this happen?" Candy demanded.

Claudia shrugged. "It's simple. One dinner party begets another, and all you have to do is catch the right dinner to start off with. Preferably before an opening night. Everybody seems to go to opening nights in New York, and that's where you do a lot of business."

"Well, I think it's wonderful," Candy approved. "Both you and David are much too young and attractive to sit home every night by yourselves the way you used to."

"I'm funny that way," said Claudia enigmatically. "I happen to like sitting home."

"So do I," Candy confessed. "John doesn't like running around either. What's gotten into David, anyway?"

It was a hard question to answer, for Candy was too young to understand the complicated mechanism of marriage. Claudia decided upon the simplest explanation. "He wants me to have the last fling," she said. "And I think," she added with narrowed eyes, "that I've about flung myself for the last time into this dress. The one good thing about the concert is that I'll be sitting down most of the evening."

"You can get lovely loose things, accordion pleated," said Candy helpfully.

"Thanks," said Claudia. "I can think of nothing I need less than accordion pleats. I'm going to have to buy a layette next week, to say nothing of a perambulator and scales and all the rest of the paraphernalia."

"Haven't you anything left from Matthew or—last time— I mean——" Candy stammered a little, not wanting to talk about the baby that hadn't lived.

"I was just about to start shopping when it happened," said

Claudia levelly, " and Matthew used up all of Bobby's things.
I haven't so much as a bellyband left."

" That's fun, beginning fresh."

" Not at this late date it's not," said Claudia. " Didn't I
manage badly, though ? Almost five years between babies."

" You couldn't help it, the war messed things up. Now
you can have a fourth one right away, and use all the stuff
over again."

Claudia shook her head. " I don't want David to work
himself to death to raise a big family. Two boys and a girl,
and I'm through."

" Then you can save the layette for me," Candy suggested
blithely. " It might be a good idea for me to go along when
you shop, so as to be sure you get the things I like."

Bobby wandered in eating a banana, with Bluster trailing
after him expectantly. " What's a layette ? " he said. " A
banana isn't dessert, it's fruit, I don't like to have supper by
myself. Why don't you and Daddy stay home any more ? "
He looked at Candy reproachfully. " Are you going out
too ? "

" I'm afraid so."

" Who with, Uncle John ? "

" Yes, he's going to drive me up to Greenwich to his house
for dinner."

" Oh shoot," said Bobby.

" I wish you wouldn't say that," Claudia reproved him.

" Daddy says it."

" That isn't what he says. He wouldn't use a naughty word
like shoot. Where's Matthew ? "

" In the bathroom. He locks the door now. What's a
layette ? "

" Tell him to unlock the door this instant—and no books."

Bobby liked nothing better than delivering orders to
Matthew. He gave Bluster the last of the banana and
vanished. Bluster accepted the banana politely, holding it in
his mouth with a blank stare before he quietly deposited it
on the carpet. Then he ambled off after Bobby.

" Oh shoot," said Claudia. Candy giggled. They were both
in the throes of hysterical merriment when Bobby came back.
" What's a layette ? " Candy hiccoughed.

" I know what it is," said Bobby curtly. " It's a baby."

Candy rolled helplessly on the bed. " Oh dear," she wept.
" Oh dear."

Claudia wiped her eyes. Matthew put in an appearance

with his pyjama bottoms falling down. He looked startled. " Why is everybody crying ? " he asked apprehensively.

" They're laughing," Bobby said in disgust, but a smirk of satisfaction lay beneath his scorn. Matthew clutched at his pyjamas and jumped up and down acting silly. Claudia could see that laughter in a room spelled the happiness and security of their world. A prayer came into her heart. " It's their right, let it always be for them——"

David came home a few minutes later. John was with him, so there was a double welcome. The children shouted as David whacked their backsides, and Candy hugged John, and Bluster barked, and Shakespeare slithered in and out, and John said, in deep appreciation, " Gosh, but this is nice and noisy." And Claudia lifted her lips for David's kiss, and thought, with a quick sinking of her heart. " He's tired tonight."

She went with him to the bedroom where his dinner clothes were laid out in readiness. He glanced in the mirror, and ran his hand over his face. " Do I have to shave ? "

" You do not," said Claudia. " You don't even have to go," she suggested hopefully. " I'll phone Julia and tell her we can't make it, and that's that."

For a moment his face lit up, and she held her breath because she thought he was going to say yes. Then it was as if a mask slipped down across his eyes. " Nonsense. Of course we'll go," he said.

While he was dressing, she followed John and Candy to the elevator. " How was David today ? " she asked casually.

" All right," John said. " Fine. Why ? "

" No special reason. Only that he coughs a little, now and then."

" Yes, I noticed that he does," said John soberly. " I imagine it's from smoking."

" I don't think so. He never used to, no matter how much he smoked. I think he never really got over his grippe properly."

" There was an epidemic at college," Candy volunteered, " and the doctor gave us some wonderful cough medicine. It was red and syrupy, and stopped it right away. I'll write up and get the name."

" No, don't," said Claudia. " David doesn't like to take medicine and he hates to be fussed over."

" I hope you realize," she told him later, as they stood waiting for the doorman to call a taxi, " how I'm not pestering you any more about your cold, and the way you don't wear your overcoat, and not eating a decent breakfast and working like a maniac, and going out nights to boot because you think it's good for me."

"Yes Ma'am," said David, at his best clowning.

He had got his second wind and was feeling better, thought Claudia. Perhaps busy people lived on their second winds. Perhaps it was good, perhaps it wasn't.

"Look," he said in deadly earnest, "do we have to sit through this whole bloody concert?"

"I'll feel faint," Claudia bargained, "if you promise to call quits on this gay life we're leading and let me stay home and go to bed early hereafter."

"For my sake," David injected with a warning note.

"No, really for mine," she assured him hastily. "Dr. Rowland doesn't want me to go out so much."

David gave a short laugh. "Doesn't he? I happen to have checked with him after your last visit, and he says it's exactly what you should be doing."

Claudia bridled. "I don't like to have you talking about me behind my back."

"Neither do I," said David, "behind mine."

He must have known why she followed John to the elevator. He was just too damn smart for words.

EIGHT

SO MANY THINGS happened after the New Year, that looking back upon the final months of her pregnancy, Claudia felt that it was like a jigsaw puzzle, with all the pieces falling into place. It began with Candy's getting married, suddenly and without any apparent reason, except a childish whim.

" Doesn't John have anything to say in the matter ? " David inquired.

" Not much," Candy admitted sunnily. " He wants to wait until he earns more money, but who wants money."

" It's nice to have," David commented.

" One of the better household conveniences," Claudia followed his lead. After all, Candy was their responsibility, and young love was hardly love at all. " It pays the rent," she added.

" There won't be any rent to pay," said Candy. " We're going to live in Greenwich with John's parents."

" You'll do nothing of the sort," said Claudia. " This is your apartment, and we'll find some other place to live. Or better yet, if you wait until Spring, we'll probably be shoving off to the North Pole."

" Don't count your chickens," David inserted, as superstitious as an actor.

" No matter if you do go, though," Candy said, " we wouldn't live here. It's much too big for us, and John doesn't want to undertake anything he can't afford. He's awfully proud when it comes to money."

" In that case," David offered carefully, " I should think you'd rather wait until you find a little place that you can swing, and go housekeeping by yourselves."

" Claudia didn't wait," Candy came back quickly. " She wasn't any older than I am, and what's more her mother lived with you and it worked out beautifully. I've often heard you say so."

" Claudia's mother was a very wonderful woman," said David gravely, leaving much unsaid. It was as if, thought Claudia with a wave of gratitude, he had removed his hat in ovation to her mother's memory. Her eyes thanked him. " David means that mothers-in-law aren't always the same as mothers or even the same as each other," she explained to

Candy gently. " Besides, it was my mother who came to live with us, and not the other way around."

" Are you trying to frighten me ? " Candy asked, with an edge of steel in her young voice. " You've never met Mrs. Payne, so I don't think it's fair to jump to conclusions that she's going to be hard to get along with. She's terribly happy to have us. She says it's wonderful not to lose John, and she's glad I'm young, because she can teach me a lot of things about making him a good wife."

" That's nice," said Claudia dubiously.

" I still want you to think twice," David urged. " People don't take marriage seriously enough any more. If they don't succeed at first, they try again. But Claudia and I don't look at it that way."

" My mother and father didn't look at it that way either," said Candy softly. " Nor John's mother and father. Nor John and I. So I think we're safe."

" I think so too," Claudia gave in gracefully.

This time it was David who followed suit. " You little brat," he said, " if I ever catch you making that partner of mine unhappy, I'll wring your neck."

" Partner ! " Candy echoed on a small bleat. " John didn't tell me ! "

" How could he tell you," said David, " when he didn't know it ? I didn't know it myself, until this minute. It's your first wedding present."

" Naughton and Payne." Candy tasted the words dreamily. " It fits together as if the names were made for each other."

" I thought the same thing," said Claudia, " when David came home ten years ago and told me that Roger had made him a junior partner in the firm. ' Killian and Naughton.' It was pretty perfect, but I think I like the sound of this partnership even better."

" It's a sort of double marriage," said Candy unsteadily. " For better or for worse, in sickness and in health, until death do us part."

A small silence fell upon them. David cleared his throat. " That's about it," he said.

The following week Candy and John were married by a Justice of the Peace. It was a quiet little ceremony with no one there except Claudia, David, and Jerry, and a sense of Elizabeth touching gently upon all of them. At the last moment, John's mother—who would have preferred a large and formal wedding—suffered a slight heart attack and had to stay home. John was so worried that Candy suggested giving up their honeymoon. As it was, he telephoned twice before they finally took off. Mrs. Payne was able to talk to him the second time, and said that she was perfectly all right, not to give her another thought.

" I wonder——" Claudia said reflectively, as they left the airport.

" Don't," David advised.

" Besides, you'll never know," Jerry added, " and neither will John."

" We're all three of us not nice," said Claudia. " You're going to stop off and have dinner with us, aren't you, Jerry ? "

" I don't think so," said Jerry. " I've been a little below par the last couple of weeks, and I'm going to pop home to bed."

" You certainly take care of yourself," Claudia remarked, " which is more than I can say for David."

" I have to," said Jerry. " I had a little flare-up this winter."

" Flare-up of what ? " asked Claudia.

Jerry looked at her, faintly surprised. " I thought Elizabeth might have mentioned it, though it isn't important, of course. I've never gone out of my way to talk about it, but I was pretty sick my senior year at college and I had to go away for three years. It's sort of played hell with my life on and off ever since."

" That was a tough break," said David soberly. " No, I never knew."

" What was Jerry talking about ? " Claudia asked, after they had dropped him off at his hotel. " You seemed to guess right away, so I didn't want to ask."

" It was fairly obvious," said David. " What does one usually go away for for three years ? "

" Oh," said Claudia, " really ? " She was momentarily stopped by the conventional image of tuberculosis that flashed across her mind, yet Jerry seemed so far removed from any actual violation of his fastidious well-being, that she found it difficult to feel more than a passing sympathy for something that happened to him so long ago. " I'm glad we can stay home alone tonight and get to bed early for a change," she said.

" Come to think of it, so am I," said David.

There wasn't much issue about the social end of their life while John was away. David left the house before eight every morning, and frequently worked through dinnertime—more often than not, Claudia suspected, having a sandwich sent in to his desk. He looked tired—he was tired—but there wasn't anything she could do about it. She protested only once, the night that Nancy Riddle telephoned after they were both asleep. Claudia could hear the excited squeak of her voice through the wires—David simply had to get up to Eastbrook the next day because she'd decided to enlarge the little salt-box house immediately. "The idea is, that I intend to simplify my whole existence," she impressed upon him. "I'll rent my big house and move into yours this spring. I don't know why I didn't think of it before ! "

David let her talk it out and that he'd call her in the morning. "I knew she'd think of it sooner or later," he remarked grimly, as he put the telephone down and lit a cigarette. "Nancy's like a drunkard when it comes to doing over houses. Anything for an excuse. She'll even live in them for a while."

" I don't care how much of a fool she is as long as you don't have to get involved," said Claudia. "What'll you do, tell her in the morning that you're too busy ? "

" I'm not too busy. I can't afford to be too busy."

" But Nancy drives you crazy," Claudia protested. "Besides, you've always liked the house exactly the way it is, and last but not least, you've already got more work than you can handle."

"We can't have too much work," said David doggedly. " The office isn't going to turn down anything from here on out, it's got to supply two livings instead of one. This won't be much of a chore, anyway. I've got the original plans, so all I have to do is sketch in the new elevations. John can draw the blueprints, and drive up with Candy every week to supervise the job."

" You make it sound very logical and easy, but I still say that life's too short to kill yourself. There's a limit to a person's strength."

" When I reach that limit, I'll let you know," said David shortly. He stomped his cigarette out, and got up to empty the ash tray in the bathroom. Then, instead of coming back to bed, he called in to her that he wasn't sleepy, he'd read in the other room for a while.

There was a note of tautness in his voice that sealed her lips. She saw an alley of light slice the hall, and narrow into darkness as he closed the door of the library so that the glow of the lamp would not disturb her. As if she could fall asleep while he was sitting in there alone, restless with some subtle torment that was destroying his peace of body and his peace of mind. She looked deep within herself to make sure that she was not at fault, that she had not roused in him another of the unpredictable moods which were growing more and more frequent. Even Bertha noticed the way he'd fly into brief explosions with the children, or the way a quick, sharp answer would escape his lips before he could hold it back. "You cannot help it, do not pay any attention," she told Claudia with a large and beautiful comprehension. "Men get that way. I have my hands full with Fritz, too. He says things he does not mean, and then right away he is sorry."

"But there's a reason for Fritz to be edgy. He's been sick for so long, no wonder."

"Yah, yah," Bertha sighed. Sorrow settled in the gentle sternness of her lips. "It is hard for a man who has always been strong and well to be suddenly on his back. Many times I wish I was the one who could be sick."

"It's so much easier," said Claudia.

It was only a short while afterwards that Fritz suffered an embolism, and died without regaining consciousness. "It is better so," said Bertha. Claudia was ashamed because it was she who wept, while Bertha remained tearless, and controlled.

"I'll go to the cemetery," said David. "It isn't necessary for you to put yourself through that kind of an ordeal now."

"I'd like not to go," Claudia confessed. "I dread it, but I think it's one of the few things that would please Bertha and Fritz—if we both went, I mean."

"Perhaps you're right," said David.

It was a beautiful funeral. There were many bouquets of bright flowers, and many friends and relatives. Claudia and David drove in the first carriage with Bertha and Edward, and Edward's children, who were Lisa's too. "Now Lisa and Papa are together," said Bertha with quiet satisfaction. "Lisa was always Papa's favourite, even though he said he had no favourite child. But when she died, something happened to him. He could not fool me, he was never the same afterwards—never."

At the grave, the grandchildren threw roses on the casket, and for the first time Bertha lowered the heavy black veil that some well-meaning cousin had tacked around her hat. On the way home she pushed it up again, and talked of other things—how nice it was that the sun came out for Fritz today, and she hoped it was not too long a trip for Claudia to have made.

" It wasn't," David assured her.

" I thank you each for going," said Bertha. " I knew Fritz liked it that you were there."

" I feel," said Claudia as they entered the apartment, " as if I'd been to church—cleansed, and peaceful, and a little awed."

" I guess that's the way a good funeral ought to make you feel," said David. He ran through the usual pile of mail on the hall table. " Nothing important," he said. " Bills, and a letter from Roger, and another invitation." He tossed her a square, white envelope, heavy as linen, and glanced through Roger's note.

" Anything important ? " Claudia asked.

" Read it."

" His writing's too small—what does he say ? "

" Just that he's holding his fingers crossed for the Iceland deal to go through, and he's flying on for a week or two this spring."

" That's nice," said Claudia. " I think of Roger quite a lot. He's a part of our old life, like Fritz and Bertha."

" I'm glad you feel that," said David. " I owe him plenty. We'll have room for him to stay with us, won't we ? "

" Provided he gets here before the baby."

" I'll write and tell him to. Who's the invitation from ? "

" I haven't looked. What's the difference, we don't have to go anyway." She opened the envelope without interest, and then laughed. " It isn't an invitation, it's an announcement."

" Of what ? "

" You'll never guess."

" Must I ? "

" Yes. Who do you think's getting married ? "

" Helen Drew, as usual."

" No, I think Helen's finished with marriage. It's Beritza."

" What the hell do I care," said David with an impatient frown.

Even the mellowing effects of a funeral wore off, thought Claudia unhappily. She knew that she was risking the fate of an entire evening but she made one more try to challenge his good temper. " But who do you think Beritza's marrying," she persisted. " You don't deserve my telling you, you're so nasty," she added hastily, as she saw that he had no intention of guessing. " It's Pinky."

She was rewarded by the reluctant grin that tugged at his lips. " For God's sake," he said.

Bobby and Matthew came home from the park a few minutes later. Katie, who had offered to take them out in Bertha's place, had bought them each a balloon. Bobby had passed the balloon stage years ago, but he pretended that he hadn't. It wasn't the kind on a string that wafted up to the ceiling either, it was a very plain balloon on a stick, which made it even harder for him to look pleased about it. " You're an awfully nice fellow," Claudia told him out of a clear sky.

" Yes, you are," said David. He studied his watch. " Let's see, it's almost five o'clock, not worth going back to the office——"

" I should say it isn't," Claudia inserted with asperity.

" Mamma, keep quiet," he ordered, " or we won't take you along."

" Along where ? " Bobby demanded.

" To the movies," said David. " We can have an early bite to eat and be home by half-past eight. How about it ? "

" Boy," said Bobby, simply. Claudia could see how relieved he was that everything was as usual—even more so—in spite of Fritz's death and the strangeness of Bertha being away. " Can Matthew come along too ? " he asked, carrying his godliness to a high point.

" Yes, Saint Bob," said Claudia. " Go stop him from taking his bath while I see what can be done about dinner."

She hurried to the kitchen, no less elated than Bobby, but for a different reason. This was the first time in weeks that David had relaxed to this degree. She couldn't get over his wanting to take the children to a movie, especially at night. He didn't believe in children going to movies any more than he believed in children answering telephones. Whatever had gotten into him though—whether it was because he thought she needed diversion after the funeral, or some unconscious reaction to Roger's approaching visit, or merely an impulse to reward Bobby for being a nice boy—she wasn't going to look a gift horse in the mouth.

It was a matter of moments to change a potential meat loaf and baked potatoes into the immediacy of hamburgers on rolls, which was practically as much nourishment and infinitely more festive. They were on their way well before six o'clock, giving them enough time to shop around from one movie house to another until, eventually, they found a picture about a deer. " I'd prefer a dog," said Claudia, " but this'll do."

They all had a soda afterwards, even David, who ordered a frosted coffee.

" What's that like ? " Matthew wanted to know before he made up his mind.

" It's a manly version of a chocolate soda, because it's coffee and the ice cream doesn't show," said Claudia. David gave her a quick little pinch for being fresh, and she almost fell off the stool, and the children laughed uproariously and made too much noise with their straws, and Claudia thought, with her heart so full that it almost choked her, " I wish I could hold the happiness of this moment forever and ever." She knew that it was asking too much, for at this very same instant, all over the world, there were people like Bertha with hearts full of sorrow.

" Finish up and let's go home," she said abruptly. " To-morrow's school."

They found Edward, sitting in the hall waiting for them, his neat dark suit full of Shakespeare's orange fur. " Bluster knew me too," he smiled.

" Why shouldn't he ? " said Claudia. " I'd never speak to them again if they didn't, the ungrateful beasts."

" Can't Edward come in and talk to us while we get undressed ? " Bobby asked.

" Yah, yah, yah ! " Matthew shouted, still wound up.

" I would like to," Edward excused himself, " but I have to get back to my job in Jersey. I hope you do not mind that I took the liberty of stopping by," he apologized to Claudia.

" Don't be silly, ' liberty,' " said Claudia.

" Come on in the living-room and have a nip of brandy," David said.

" Please, no thank you. I just got up from a big dinner at Bertha's house."

" All the more reason," said David.

In the end, he took some sherry, holding the small wine-glass carefully between his work-scarred fingers. " I am sorry to bother you like this," he began with a nervous clearing of his throat. " But there is something I wanted to talk to you about."

" Where do you get all these ridiculous words like ' liberty ' and ' bother,' " said David. " We don't have to stand on ceremony with each other. We've been through too much together. Including the little matter of a war."

"You fought the war, I only stayed behind," said Edward. He glanced down at his right hand with its missing finger. "That is something a man does not forget too soon."

"I couldn't have gotten through those years without you," Claudia told him.

"I miss the old farm," he said sadly.

"You might miss it," said David, "but our giving it up was a good break for you. Full charge of one of the most important strings of Guernseys in the country is quite a thing."

"It's a fine position," Edward granted, "and now that I am settled, I think I should take over the charge of my children from Bertha, and have them with me."

"I don't quite see how that'll work out," said David. "Aren't you living with the chauffeur's family?"

"Yes, but that is not a good arrangement," Edward explained. "There's a separate tenant cottage on the estate for the head herdsman, and the only thing the boss did not like when he hired me was that I was not a married man—I mean that I did not have a wife to keep house for me. But Lisa is a grown-up girl now, her grandmother has taught her how to cook and keep things tidy, and there's no reason why we could not take the little cottage together. There is also a school for the boy, with a bus service passing in front of our door."

"In that case, it sounds very feasible," said David.

"Neither of you seem to realize," Claudia demurred, "that's it's going to be hard on Bertha to be left alone now. She'll miss the children terribly. Especially Lisa."

"That is the reason I came to see you," said Edward. "Bertha does not know I am here, she would be angry with me. But I have talked to her about her plans, and she thinks certainly I should take the children—I know what is in her heart, you see."

It was in Claudia's heart too, but she hadn't dared to voice it. "Bertha wants to come back——" she breathed.

Edward nodded. "Only she thinks you do not need her because you already have two maids."

"But she knows they're only on loan with the apartment," Claudia protested. "She also knows that Katie's planning to go back to Ireland this spring. What's the matter with that woman, anyway?"

"She is afraid of one thing," said Edward. "She is afraid maybe you might feel she is too old to take care of a new baby."

"She's crazy," said David. "Go call her, Claudia."

"She's not only crazy," said Claudia, on her way to the telephone, "she's stark staring mad."

NINE

BERTHA SAID it would take her about three weeks to settle Fritz' small insurance, and dispose of her household furnishings. Katie was very pleased at this turn of events. "Then I will stay on," she told Claudia, "until Bertha comes. It'll give me time to get a permanent wave, and go to the dentist and do a lot of other things I have to do before my boat sails."

"That couldn't be better," said Claudia, "because that means you'll still be here when Mr. Killian comes on from California. He's going to stay with us for a few days, and I'd like everything to be awfully nice—the best towels and sheets, and I think he likes finger bowls at night and all that sort of thing."

Katie nodded her head slowly up and down. "I know Mr. Roger," she said. "He used to come quite often in the old days, being Mrs. Van Doren's cousin and all. A lovely gentleman."

"Yes, of course, I didn't realize you'd been with Mrs. Van Doren that long."

"I remember when poor Mr. Roger got his divorce, too," said Katie. "I never cared so much for Mrs. Killian, she never understood him. I always said to myself, 'there's a man that's too fine for the average woman.'"

Claudia smiled at Katie's instinctive sizing-up of Roger. It was one of the seven wonders of the world that he and David had been so close, both as friends and partners, but there it was. In the final analysis, David probably had more understanding and appreciation than the average woman—possibly because he wasn't a woman. "I don't think I should have liked to have been married to Roger myself," Claudia decided. Still, he was as Katie put it, a lovely gentleman, and she found herself looking forward to his visit. She planned a small dinner party for his first night—Candy and John, and Julia and Hartley and Jerry. "Was Roger ever very intimate with the Dexters?" she asked David.

"No," said David, "not particularly. Have Beritza and Pinky instead. They're not my taste, but they'll be much more amusing to Roger."

"I see what you mean," said Claudia.

It was she who took the telephone call from the coast, a

week or two later. She thought nothing of it when the operator told her that Los Angeles was calling—it was undoubtedly Roger, verifying his arrival within the next few days. At first, indeed, she thought that it was Roger's voice—she remembered how beautifully he always chiselled his words.

"This is George Davidson, a friend of Roger Killian's——" Even so, she thought nothing of it. Roger was already on his way East, most likely—and his friend was letting her know.

"*Roger was taken to the hospital last night. He died on the operating table.*"

David came home from the office a little later. She wanted to break the news to him gently, but all control had deserted her. She was conscious of an amazement that Roger's death should have affected her so deeply. "I haven't laid eyes on him for years," she sobbed. "I don't know why I should feel like this."

"Cry it out," said David. "It's good for you."

"First Fritz, and now Roger. It seems that everybody that had to do with our life is dying off."

"A lot of people complain about that," said David. "It's the toll for growing old."

"When I told Katie," Claudia gulped, "she said that she never knew it to fail, deaths always came in threes——"

"Katie's a nice old ignorant jackass," said David.

"So am I."

"No darling, you're just pregnant." He gave her his handkerchief so that she could blow her nose. After she blew it, he put his arms around her. "You're going to have a baby, remember?"

"Do you think that's why I'm so wishy-washy?" she besought him.

"I think so."

"I hope so," she amended.

On a morning not long afterwards, Bertha appeared upon the scene with all her earthly belongings packed into a single, old-fashioned valise. Two pictures, face down, were laid carefully between the folds of the old nurse's cape that Bertha had worn when Matthew was a baby. Julia, with her talent for knowing what people wanted, had given it to her for a Christmas present. "Such beautiful material," said Bertha, tenderly, as she lifted it out. "Many times I wanted to cut it up for a coat for little Lisa, but always I thought, 'No, I will keep it. Maybe some day I will use it again.'"

" It's as good as new," Claudia marvelled, " and you always looked so stylish in it and made us feel so rich."

" I have the veil that went with it too," said Bertha. " It is packed at the bottom." She stood in the middle of the floor, looking for a place to put her two pictures—one of Fritz when he was young, and the other of Lisa in her wedding gown. " This is all I have now," she said, without rebellion.

" I think they'd look lovely on the dressing table," Claudia suggested softly.

" Yes," said Bertha. " It's such a beautiful piece of furniture. I will be very careful of it. Miss Candy will want it when she goes housekeeping for herself. She doesn't mind my using it ? "

" No, it was her idea to use her old room for a nursery, on account of the southern exposure."

" It is wonderful," said Bertha. " So full of sunshine. The baby and I should be very happy in here."

Claudia could feel her soul stretch up to touch Bertha's lofty height. " It takes such courage to build a new life from scratch," she said to David that evening. " I don't think I ever could."

" You under-estimate yourself."

" After the way I carried on about Roger ?   Don't flatter me."

" Oh, I don't know," said David, weighing it, " it seems to me that you've handled the few hard knocks in your life pretty well so far."

" There haven't really been any.   Just scares."

" One day we're bound to have the real thing," he said, " and I'll lay even bets that you'll come through."

" I wish you wouldn't talk that way."

" Why should we be any different from anyone else ? " he argued reasonably. " Did my grey suit come back from the cleaners ? "

" Not yet."

" Hell."

" Can't you wear your pink instead ? "

" This is no joke, it's been out two weeks."

" One.   It only seems like two."

He gave her an affectionate rumple. " You're feeling pretty well, these days, aren't you ? "

" So are you," she said, happily.

" I always felt all right."

" But you coughed, and you looked awful. Now you hardly cough at all, and your colour's a lot better, you look fine."

"That's because we've had so much happening around here that you haven't had time to pester me. I'm like the unwatched pot."

Like an idiot, she believed him. It wasn't until after the baby came that she found out about the bottle of patent cough mixture that he kept in his desk at the office, and the sunlamp treatments at the barber's. It was easy to fool her those last weeks of her pregnancy, with nature making birth the goal of life. David hid the newspaper that carried an account of Edith Dexter's suicide from an overdose of sleeping pills (though when Claudia eventually heard about it, she thought, with a pang of mingled sorrow and relief, " there goes Katie's third death "). He didn't tell her about Jerry either, who pulled up stakes following an attack of so-called bronchitis, and went to Mexico to live for good. He didn't even tell her about herself—that Dr. Rowland wasn't satisfied with the way things looked. " Keep her very quiet this last month," he warned David, " but don't frighten her by making it serious."

April came and David relaxed. " Now you can turn somersaults for all I care," he said.

" I'm glad I didn't know there was any danger of the baby coming earlier," she admitted. " After what happened last time, I'd have been terrified."

" I was a little terrified myself," said David.

The pains began quite normally, early on a Monday afternoon. Bertha had taken Matthew to the park, and Bobby was staying in school for the rehearsal of an Easter play. It was the sort of set-up that Claudia had always dreamed of, but babies—her babies, anyway—had always chosen Sunday morning or the middle of the night to start, and then taken most of the following day to finish up. " This seems to be going to be different," she exulted. " This is going to be neat, quick, and to the point."

She closed the door of her bedroom, and notified Dr. Rowland's office that she was leaving for hospital right away. On the way out, she stuck her head in the kitchen where Mary was drying the lunch dishes. " If by any chance Mr. David should telephone again, tell him I've gone to the beauty parlour to have my hair washed," she said.

" I could wash it for you," Mary offered.

"Thanks, but I need a manicure, too. Oh, by the way," she added carelessly, "I haven't a definite appointment, so I might have to wait around ; tell Bertha when she comes that she shouldn't worry if I'm late."

"I'll tell her," said Mary.

Bluster followed hopefully to the door. "No, no," said Claudia. "You can't come." She bent to kiss his great, silly head. "Whatever you do, don't tell anybody I took a suitcase," she whispered.

Except for the pains it was fun. The taxi driver was wonderful to her, and told her that his wife had just had twins, both girls, but one had died.

"Oh dear," said Claudia, and thought how true it was that haste makes waste. "I'll take one girl and like it," she decided.

There was the usual red tape at the admission desk, even though this was her fourth visit to the same hospital, including her appendix. A plump little probationer, with more than petticoats beneath her voluminous blue-striped skirt, finally appeared to escort her up to the maternity floor. As she bustled along, with her hand cupped superfluously beneath Claudia's elbow, she volunteered the information that her name was Miss Zink—but everybody called her Inky—and she was going to stay right on the case until the Special came. "We're very short of Specials," she said, "but don't worry, Dr. Rowland's an awfully big shot around here, and he'll manage to get someone for you."

"He doesn't have to bother," said Claudia, "I don't need a Special Nurse. I don't need a corner room either," she added, as Inky led her to the end of the corridor and opened a door. The room had two expensive windows. "And a private bath," she discovered in short order.

Inky nodded. "Yes, indeedy, it's the best room on the floor."

"That's exactly it," said Claudia. She knew from past experience that although Dr. Rowland was nice about his initial fee because of Julia, his upkeep was high just the same. It was a point of pride with him for his patients to enjoy the best of everything.

"Please see if I can see Dr. Rowland right away," she said.

"Oh no," Inky protested, "I'm not to call him until you're three minutes apart." She peered at her watch. "Tell me when your next pain comes."

"I'm not going to have any more pains in this room," said

laudia firmly. As luck would have it, a pain slipped up on
er and closed her mouth. Inky rushed to the bureau and
ithdrew from the bottom drawer a rough cotton gown with
rings at the back. "Of course you can wear a pretty one of
our own after it's all over," she suggested, "but this kind is
uch more convenient while it's going on. Now I'll help you
ndress, and you get straight into bed."

Claudia stood as pat as she could, under the circumstances.
No!" she repeated stubbornly. "Why should I have a
rivate bath I can't ever use."

"It comes with the room," Inky pointed out helplessly.

"I want a room that nothing comes with," Claudia insisted.
Just one window and a bed."

Inky looked a little frightened. "Now don't excite your-
elf," she said soothingly. "It won't be any extra if you use
he bed in this room for a little. Really, now, we have to get
usy."

Getting busy, as Inky phrased it, was one of the things
Claudia liked least about having a baby. Inky wasn't very
experienced at it, either. "This is my very first obstetrical
case," she announced proudly.

"Hurray," said Claudia, wincing. If she had to have a
Special, she wished she could have had her at this stage of the
game. There was no point in paying her just to sit by the
window and do crossword puzzles. By the time Dr. Rowland
put in his appearance, however, she had lost all interest in
discussing economy. "Where's your husband?" he inquired
at once. "I didn't see him outside."

"I don't want him to know anything at all until the baby's
here."

"Why?" asked Dr. Rowland blankly.

She didn't have the breath to explain, and he wouldn't have
understood anyway. "Promise not to call him!" she gasped.

She felt like a fool because no sooner had Dr. Rowland
left the room, than David marched in big as life, and looking
very smug. "So," he said, "you're getting a manicure and a
shampoo, are you?"

"That good-for-nothing miserable dog!" cried Claudia.

Inky thought she meant Dr. Rowland, and said "Oh!"
Claudia explained that it was her Great Dane who must have
told on her, and Inky looked more startled than ever and
hurriedly left the room. "She's going to write on my chart
that I'm irrational," said Claudia. "How did you find out
anyway, David? You've ruined my whole fun."

" I'm glad you think it's fun."

" Go on, tell me how you knew."

" Well," said David, " I decided you were up to no goo
when Mary gave me your message about the beauty parlou
It didn't sound natural, so I called Dr. Rowland's office an
talked to his nurse."

" Very smart. I didn't expect you to telephone home agair
Why did you ? "

" To tell you not to wait dinner. Nancy Riddle blew int
town. Guess what she wants now ? Georgian columns o
a salt-box house."

" Serves you right, I told you not to begin with her. Di
you tell her I was in the hospital ? "

" Of course."

" I hope she doesn't send me fruit."

" I've got to see her tomorrow," said David, " and I'll d
what I can about it."

" And do something else while you're about it," said Claudia
urgently, trying to get it in ahead of a pain, " change my room
while I'm upstairs. It's sheer and utter waste to have a private
bath, it'll only make me nervous to see it standing there."

" I'll use it," David promised, " I'll take a bath every
evening when I come. Will that make you feel happier about
it ? "

She managed a smile before she bit her lips. He reached
for a towel and gently wiped her forehead. It was getting to
be less and less fun every minute. She wished she could have
spared him, but she was beginning to be glad that he was there.

She knew that he was still there when they brought her down
from the delivery room. She knew, too, that things hadn't
gone as well as they should have, but the only thing that
mattered was that the baby was alive. She had heard him
cry, and she had heard Dr. Rowland say that it was a fine big
boy. She wanted to tell him he had made a mistake, it was
a girl, not a boy, but she kept drifting off into a vast
nothingness, full of quiet pain.

" What time is it ? " she asked, without opening her eyes.

" Half-past nine."

Her lids had heavy weights on them. The light in the room
helped her to lift them. " It must be half-past nine in the
morning," she figured out with effort.

" Yes, you've had a nice long sleep. Your son is waiting
to see you."

The voice attached itself to a nurse. The nurse was bending over her. Claudia saw that she wore a white uniform—the Special, doubtless—who had slipped in like a snake in the grass while her back was turned. " My name is Miss Bates," she introduced herself, and added, a trifle accusingly, " Dr. Rowland took me off another case to come to you."

" Thank you," said Claudia, politely. " I mean thank him, but he needn't have bothered. Did you say I had a son ? " she asked after a moment.

" Nine pounds and two ounces."

Claudia thought about it. Her mind felt bulky, as if layers of cotton were packed inside her brain. " That's a pretty big baby," she decided at length. " How did I ever do it ? "

" Not too easily," said Miss Bates succinctly. " That's why you've got to be extremely careful for a day or two."

The whole thing was peculiar, Claudia reflected. She had been so sure that everything was going to go so fast and be simple and that the baby would be a girl. Life was certainly fresh with her all of a sudden. She hoped David hadn't had too hard a time of it last night and that he wasn't disappointed in not having a daughter. " Has my husband been here this morning ? " she asked.

" Not yet."

" I'd like to telephone him."

" There'll be no telephoning," said Miss Bates.

" But I won't be able to sleep unless I do."

" It's against orders."

" It'll do me more harm than good if you don't," Claudia threatened, " so you'd better let me."

Miss Bates frowned as she read the handwriting on the wall. " I see where you're going to be a difficult patient," she said.

" Very," Claudia agreed. " You'll wish you'd stayed with your other case."

Bertha answered the telephone, choked with excitement. " I am glad it is a boy," she said defiantly, " I wanted a boy all the time."

" So did I, now that I have it," said Claudia. " Where's Mr. David ? "

" I think he went down to the office already."

" You think ? Don't you know ? "

Bertha sounded flustered. " Yes, I am sure of it," she said. " Surely he went to the office."

" But surely he's going to stop in at the hospital first ? " Claudia demanded.

4

" He will be surely there later today."

" Well I should surely hope so," Claudia retorted. The cotton was gone from her brain, her mind was clear as a bell, and she felt in excellent form. " I have to make one more call," she said, warding Miss Bates away. " I feel fine."

" You do not feel fine," Miss Bates contradicted flatly. " The morphine has had an overstimulating effect upon you."

" Goody," said Claudia, reaching for the instrument.

" This is outrageous," Miss Bates exclaimed. " It's the worst possible thing for your milk, too ! "

" Nonsense," said Claudia. " My milk won't be in for three days. I know all about it, I'm an old hand at the business."

It was too early for David's secretary to be in the office, but John had already come in. He sounded as excited as Bertha when he heard her voice. " Claudia ! What are you doing on the phone, you amaze me ! You had everybody worried to death last night ! It's wonderful about the baby —you know you're the sort of person who should always have boys. Candy and I will come racing to see you as soon as we're allowed to——"

" Any time," said Claudia, struggling to get a word in edgewise. It almost seemed as if he didn't want to give her a chance to talk—he didn't sound at all like himself. " I'd like to speak to David," she said.

" David ? He's not here."

" That's funny—Bertha said he'd left for the office, and he hasn't been to the hospital, so I wonder where he can be ? "

" I think he's meeting Nancy Riddle somewhere," said John. " I believe they're having lunch together."

" Oh," said Claudia. She was suddenly very tired. Miss Bates was right, she did not feel at all fine. She lay back on her pillows, trying to put two and two together, and getting nowhere. It was entirely plausible that David had met Nancy at her hotel, but it was inconceivable that he had not stopped off at the hospital first, or even telephoned. " Please go out to the desk and see if Mr. Naughton didn't come while I was asleep, or whether he hasn't left some message for me," she implored Miss Bates.

" I should think you'd be asking for your baby," Miss Bates remarked.

" I'll take more interest in him after I find out where my husband is."

" I see," said Miss Bates slowly. She didn't see at all, but she thought she did. She lost no time in finding out whether

Mr. Naughton had made any effort whatsoever to check on his wife's condition, and returned with the information that the hospital had seen neither hide nor hair of him since eleven o'clock the previous night. "And if he had telephoned, the message would have been left at the desk," Miss Bates finished up with a sympathetic cluck.

"He'll probably come in after he leaves Nancy Riddle," said Claudia.

Miss Bates gave another cluck, this time an intensely censorious one, and straightened Claudia's pillows. "Never mind," she said, "you just put your thoughts on that sweet little son of yours. I'm going to bring him right in to you right away."

The baby was no better and no worse than any new-born baby, except that he had quite a pompadour of black hair, which Claudia knew from past experience didn't mean a thing. He was probably big next to the other babies in the nursery, but all alone, wrapped up in a voluminous blue blanket, he seemed very average. "He's a wonderful, wonderful little boy," Miss Bates prompted encouragingly. "Look at that cunning little mouth, will you, and that dear little button of a nose, and all that *hair,* if you please ! "

"I am," said Claudia obediently.

Eventually, having failed to make the accepted emotional contact between mother and child, Miss Bates bore the baby away again. Then she came back and gave Claudia a sponge bath, took her temperature, and made her swallow a small tumbler of unpleasant liquid which she remembered from Matthew and Bobby.

Somewhere, far off in the city, a whistle blew for twelve o'clock. Miss Bates said that Claudia could have anything she wanted to eat—within reason—and wouldn't a nice poached egg just touch the spot ? Claudia said she had no spot, and turned her face to the wall. "Mercy, this will never, never do," Miss Bates cried. "You're just making yourself ill."

"I promise to eat after my husband comes," said Claudia. "But it would only stick in my throat now and not do me a bit of good. Please go out to the desk again and see if he hasn't telephoned. He's bound to before he goes out to lunch with Mrs. Riddle. I'm sure he'd want to leave word where he could be reached."

"Very well, my dear, but don't build your hopes," said Miss Bates. "I gave orders to switch all messages to the room, because I know how upset you are. Not that I blame you," she remarked under her breath, as she stalked from the room. Claudia could tell that she hadn't ever liked men very much anyway, and at this added example of their perfidy, she liked them less than ever.

She came back in a few minutes, with no message but carrying instead a great basket of fruit tented with a shiny blue paper, and tied around with flat red string. "Look what just came for you," she opened up brightly. "Isn't it simply scrumptious ? "

"I don't know yet," said Claudia, "until you take the paper off."

"I mean the *size* of it," Miss Bates explained.

"That only means that there's a pineapple in the bottom," said Claudia bitterly. "And when there's a pineapple in the bottom, there are always prunes in all the little gold packages stuck around. Not nuts, or candies, or little jars of jelly. Just prunes."

Miss Bates had no answer to such complete defeatism. She tore off the wrappings, and gave a little gasp of admiration. "Isn't that lovely, did you ever *see* such enormous apples and oranges ! And look at that peach, it doesn't look *real* ! Where's the card—oh here it is——"

"You'd better put it in one of the small bureau drawers," said Claudia, "so that we can keep everything together until I get around to thanking people."

"But don't you want to look first who sent the fruit ? "

"I don't have to look, Mrs. Riddle sent it," said Claudia wearily.

"Oh," said Miss Bates. She held the card between her thumb and first finger with distaste, and turned toward the bureau. "Wait a minute," Claudia stopped her. "Maybe I'd better be sure." She remembered suddenly that David had promised to try to get Nancy off of fruit, and it was barely possible that the basket was from Candy's mother-in-law, or Julia's aunt. Certain types of unimaginative women always sent food of some kind to hospitals, regardless of the fact that you could get all you wanted for nothing—like baths. She slipped the little square of parchment out of its envelope, but as soon as she saw the loose uphill scrawl, she knew that Nancy had stuck to her guns. "Congratulations," Nancy wrote. "Will try to see you when I get into town again. Sorry to hear David is ill. Hope nothing serious. As ever, Nancy."

Twice before—once when David was in an automobile accident, and again, during the war—Claudia had had this sense of doom crashing down upon her. Miss Bates' brusque voice came to her from far away. " Now see here, Mrs. Naughton, no more bouncing around, you're to lie back and be quiet, you're as white as a ghost."

Claudia tried to explain that something was wrong with David, he was ill, and there was a conspiracy to keep it from her, but in the middle of it her teeth began to chatter, and the whole bed shook with a chill. Miss Bates didn't know that it was a nervous chill. She ran to get hot water bottles, and sent out an emergency call for Dr. Rowland.

TEN

WHILE YOU WERE having a chill, Claudia discovered, you couldn't do much else than have it. David was right there in front of her mind, but she couldn't get to him through the shaking.

Suddenly it was over, and Miss Bates peeled off the blankets and took away the hot water bottles. As soon as she left the room with them, Claudia leaned over to get the telephone. The table seemed a long distance to lean to, and the instrument had become very heavy all at once, as if it were nailed down. She was struggling with it when the door opened. She started guiltily, and flopped back on her pillows with her eyes closed, pretending that she hadn't been up to anything except turning on her side. David's voice said, "Hey, there, what's the idea of fooling me, you're not asleep !"

Her eyes flew open. There he was, standing in front of her, perfectly well and whole as far as she could tell, but wearing that skinned pale look of a new haircut which he certainly couldn't have had the time to have. "David !" she cried, and out of sheer relief, burst into silly tears. "Darling, darling"—he besought her—"what is it, tell me what's wrong——"

"You didn't come," she blubbered. "You never even phoned—I got so frantic——"

He was kneeling by the bed, his arms around her. "But you foolish girl, I told you I had to see Nancy this morning."

At this juncture, Miss Bates walked in and heard what David said, and saw Claudia's tears. She got red spots on her neck and walked out again, her starched flat backside swishing with disapproval.

David stared after her. "Is that your nurse ?"

"Yes."

"What's the matter with her ? Why didn't she talk to me ?"

"She doesn't care to talk to you. She thinks you're running around with another woman, and breaking my heart."

"At least I tell you the truth about it. She ought to give me that much credit."

Claudia fished beneath the pillow and handed him Nancy's

card. " So you tell me the truth, you spent the morning with Nancy," she accused him.

He got to his feet, the image of Bobby, the way he stood there squirming. " All right, if you must know it," he admitted finally, " I stayed in bed this morning. Better men than I am have collapsed under the strain of having a baby."

" That doesn't hold water. This happens to have been your third child. I didn't notice you collapsing with the first two."

" It's the repetition that's getting me down," he said.

He intended to pass it all off as a joke, but even so he could not dispel the fear that gnawed into her throat. " David, don't try to fool me," she begged. " You can't, anyway."

" I know. You'd have made a great career as a detective."

She smiled faintly. " That's what Mamma used to say— don't think I like being that way," she broke off tensely. " I wish I was the kind that could be fooled. It would save me no end of agony."

He bent over to lay his cheek against her hair. " I'm sorry, darling, I really don't blame you for getting stewed up, and dammit, I should have gotten here earlier, but I couldn't make it."

His confession crystallized her fears. " What was it ? "

" Malaria. A nasty attack of it just when I thought I was shed of the blasted thing."

" Are you sure that's all it was ? "

" I ought to know the symptoms by this time."

" You should have called Dr. Mack anyway," she insisted perversely.

" When I call that pompous monkey." he said, " you can send for the undertaker at the same time."

" David, stop it, that kind of talk isn't at all good for my milk ! "

" Look, it wasn't a bad attack," he hastened to assure her. " Not much of a headache, and the fever broke in a couple of hours in a sweat."

" You never had a sweat before."

" Well, this was a good one," he bragged. " Bertha heard me get up around five, and came in and changed the sheets for me. Then I fell asleep, and would you believe it, I slept until a little while ago. Bertha should have wakened me."

" I'm glad she didn't. You must have been exhausted, anyway. Did Bertha know when I telephoned this morning that you wouldn't be able to come over ? "

" Yes. She said you caught her with her pants down. Only

she didn't say 'pants down.' Luckily she had already tele
phoned John before you called him, so he made up the stor
about Nancy."

"I noticed that they both sounded a little funny, but
thought they were excited on account of the baby."

"What about the baby ? " David remembered belatedly
" Where is he ? I didn't catch more than a glimpse of him
last night. Homely little devil. What are we going to cal
him ? "

"They're all homely at first—wouldn't you be ? I wish
we'd put a little more thought on boy's names. In the long
run I suppose we can't go wrong on Michael, it's safer than
Timothy or Peter or Anthony or any of the other names
floating around on children these days."

"Michael it is," said David. "Let's get back to you." He
eyed her critically. "How do you feel ? "

"I just had a chill," she said modestly.

He looked concerned. "That's not too bright."

"It's as bright as you were with your malaria," she
retorted.

"I didn't pull a lot of monkey business the way you did last
night though," he said soberly.

She was intrigued. "Real monkey business ? "

"Real monkey business. For about a half an hour we
didn't know whether you were going to come through it or
not."

She was genuinely shocked. "Was it as bad as that ? Oh
David, it would have been too awful if something had
happened to this baby after last time."

"It wasn't the baby that worried us. It was you."

"Me ? You mean I could have really died ? "

"More or less." He spoke half jokingly, but his hand
reached for hers, and held it so tight that her wedding ring
cut her finger. The pain told her more than his lips. For all
his emancipated talk, he was as dependent upon her as she
was upon him. The only difference was that he didn't show
it as much.

Dr. Rowland came a few minutes later. "What's this Miss
Bates tells me about a chill," he began immediately, as he
lifted Claudia's wrist. "You seem to be feeling pretty fit as
far as I can see. Pulse a little rapid, but good quality. Any
aches or pains anywhere ? "

"None," said Claudia. "I think it was just nerves. I was
worried about David."

Dr. Rowland eyed David with a slight lift of his brows. "So I heard," he remarked. "The nurse said your wife has been upset about you all day."

"Yes, I picked a fine time to have an attack of malaria," said David.

Dr. Rowland said, "Oh," and added speculatively, "You do look a little peaked. What have you been taking as a suppressive, quinine or atabrin?"

"Neither for the last few months," said David. "I thought I was over it."

"He's always thinking he's over things," Claudia injected, shamelessly making the most of Dr. Rowland's professional ear. "He had the flu the beginning of the winter, and he was over it the next day."

Dr. Rowland missed the ironic overtone. "You were luckier than I was," he said. "I was in bed two weeks with the damn bug, went to Florida to recuperate, got a relapse down there, and was laid up for another two weeks."

Claudia could see David puff up like a balloon. "I hope you're satisfied," he said.

"I'm not," said Claudia, stubbornly.

David rolled his eyes with his shoulders. "Doctor Rowland, will you tell this wife of mine that she's got to quit worrying about other people and take care of herself for a change?"

"I most certainly will," Dr. Rowland obliged, but before he could say anything more, Miss Bates stuck her head in at the door and announced, in a tight voice, that Mrs. Naughton's sister-in-law was in the hall. "I told her that you've given orders that there are to be no visitors, Doctor, but she said to tell you she's leaving for Bermuda in the morning."

While Dr. Rowland hesitated, Claudia could see his mind work—Julia happened to be one of his best patients, and although he was primarily a gynecologist, he kept a hand in Hartley's highly lucrative gall-bladder as well. "I'll make an exception," he decided. "Tell me," he asked Claudia in an intimate aside, as he helped himself to a grape from Nancy's basket of fruit, "is she still interested in this occult fad of hers?"

"Julia doesn't call it a fad," said Claudia. "She says she's had some wonderful experiences."

David gave a grunt which Dr. Rowland took as a signal to express his own views on the subject. "It's too bad," he

said. " It's just too bad, that a capable woman like that with
a level business head and her feet on the ground, should get
in the hands of a charlatan and lose her balance completely."

Claudia wanted to venture the opinion that Julia had
probably lost too many organs with her operation, but Dr.
Rowland might have taken it as a criticism of an over-zealous
scalpel. Besides, Julia was already in the room. Though
very thin, she looked extremely well, almost beautiful, with
the luminous glow of a woman who had just come from
meeting a lover. Dr. Rowland commented on the fact with
distrust. Julia gave her small, private laugh, so full of inner
exhilaration, and said, " I'll tell you all about it one of these
days."

Dr. Rowland picked up his bag. " I'll have to be getting
along," he said. " I'm due at the clinic," and David added
quickly, " I'll walk down the hall with you."

Julia didn't seem to notice the alacrity with which they
departed from the room. She drew up a chair to the side
of the bed and sat forward with her hands clasped intently.
" I've just come from the most remarkable sitting," she said.
" ' V ' came through and told me that you'd had quite a time
of it last night, and that he'd been with you during the whole
ordeal to give you strength."

" That was awfully nice of him," said Claudia, somewhat
taken aback, for it was rather embarrassing to learn that a
strange spirit had been hovering over her while she was on
the delivery table. She had an overwhelming desire to inquire
whether ' V ' had seen her mother anywhere around, but
David's grunt echoed in her ears, and harnessed her to sanity.
" Did ' V ' say anything about David's malaria ? " she asked
instead.

" Not about malaria particularly, but he did say that David
was in a transitional period, and would have to go through a
great deal before things finally settled for him."

It sounded a little frightening. Claudia turned it over in
her mind with apprehension. " What kind of a 'great
deal ' ? "

" I don't know," said Julia. " We aren't given things
literally ; symbolism plays a large part, and sometimes we
can't interpret what is told us until long afterwards."

" That leaves an awfully wide leeway," Claudia commented,
" you can read anything into anything."

" According to one's own understanding and development,
that's very true," Julia agreed softly. " It's almost a test of

one's spiritual capacity." She smiled. "Of course I realize that you're interested mainly in the immediate future, and 'V' did mention again that you and David would be going to a cold climate."

Claudia started to remind her that Iceland was not overly cold, but it seemed niggling to do so. She wished she shared Julia's willingness to believe. Or perhaps it was a need to believe, for being married to a man like David was an entirely different matter from being married to a man like Hartley. A man like David took up all of a woman's slack. In all modesty, she supposed it worked the other way around too. "David and I are the luckiest people in the world," she said aloud. It followed Julia's last remark quite consistently, so Julia conceded that the commission would be a wonderful break professionally. "Although from your point of view," she said, "I shouldn't like to pick up stakes and trot off to Iceland with a large family."

"It does scare me a little," Claudia confessed. "But David says he won't have to be there more than six months at the most."

"In that case, why don't you stay on here, as long as Candy isn't using the apartment? If you had no children, it might be different."

"It's partly because we have got children," Claudia started to explain, and then she realized that Julia would never understand the importance of being a family. "I couldn't live without David," she summed up briefly. "Even for six months."

"What about David, perhaps he'd welcome a vacation from domesticity?"

Claudia shook her head. "I don't think he'd like living without me either."

"My, what an old-fashioned marriage," Julia laughed. "You never have any regrets, do you?" she digressed curiously.

"Regrets!"

"Oh, not about marrying David. I mean the shaping of your own life."

"I've shaped my life."

"That's just it," said Julia. "Jim Varney was at the house for dinner a couple of nights ago, and he told me that if you'd kept on acting, you'd have really gone some place."

"It didn't happen to be the place I wanted to go to," said Claudia.

Julia shrugged. "Then that's my answer. By the way, 'V' said he'd like to talk to you sometime. When you're up and around, perhaps you'll go to a sitting with me."

"Perhaps." (Over David's dead body, Claudia amended silently.) Was Julia so bewitched that she couldn't see that her precious "V" was looking for business behind the lips of some unscrupulous medium? It was a strain to keep from saying what she really thought about the whole setup, and she was glad when the door opened and Hartley tiptoed in, effectively putting an end to the conversation. Julia reached for her light fur cape—Julia had furs for every season of the year, including summer. "Hello, dear," she said. "We have to go to a reception for Lord and Lady Argyle," she explained to Claudia.

"It sounds stuffy," said Claudia. "Hello, Hartley."

"Damned nuisance," said Hartley, and added in a whisper, "Hello, Claudia. I saw David and the doctor outside——"

"You can talk out loud," said Claudia. "What were David and Dr. Rowland doing?"

"They were admiring the baby. Handsome little fellow. They said I could pop in and see you for a minute. How are you?"

"Fine," said Claudia.

"You look fine," said Hartley.

"You look fine too," said Claudia. It was really true. Hartley's ruddy complexion never failed him, and his body had accommodated itself with a certain amount of ease to the approaching portliness of middle age. An expensive tailor had a lot to do with it, of course, but even so, Hartley was good-looking enough to be worthy of being David's brother. David was entitled to nice-looking relatives. She reached her hand toward him in a sudden impulse of affection. He seemed touched and a little at a loss and said, for want of something better, "This is the same room I had when I was here with my gall-bladder."

"It couldn't be, dear," Julia said pleasantly. "This is the maternity floor."

"Then it was the corner room directly below," said Hartley.

"Directly above," Julia corrected. She brushed her lips against Claudia's cheek. "We'd better let you rest now, we'll see you when we get back from Bermuda. And I forgot to tell you, I ordered a lovely grey perambulator, and we've left a standing order for flowers for as long as you're in the hospital."

" Oh, thanks ! " Claudia exclaimed from the bottom of her heart. Julia and Hartley certainly had their good points.

It wasn't until the end of the week that Bertha brought Bobby and Matthew to the hospital, and Claudia wasn't too anxious to see them even then. David's short visits, morning and evening, reassured her that he was well again, but very often it was an effort to pull herself out of the smothering blanket of pain that separated her from the world of reality. On the day that the children came, she asked for a hand mirror, and stared at herself and said, " I look awful."

Bertha must have thought she looked pretty awful too, because her first words were, " Ach, you look wonderful." She pushed Bobby and Matthew toward the bed. " Say nicely Hello to your Mamma——"

" Hello," they said nicely, but with discomfiture.

" Hello," said Claudia. She made no further effort to re-establish their relationship, for she knew that she would remain a stranger to them until she was up and around again. " Have some candy," she followed up casually, " it's on the bureau."

They were so relieved that they didn't have to behave with sick-room etiquette that she made up her mind not to subject them to the strain of meeting the baby and asking them how it felt to have a darling little brother. " You go out and see him in the nursery," she suggested to Bertha in an undertone. Bertha glanced at the children ; she felt that the thing to do was to take them along with her, but they were absorbed in hazarding the inside of a chocolate from its outside. " It's that green stuff," Bobby decided. " You take it."

" Can I have two ? " Matthew inquired, playing safe.

" *May* I have two ? " Claudia corrected, bestowing a broad wink on Bobby, to whom this grammatical routine was an old story.

" May I have two ? " Matthew complied.

" No, dear, you mayn't ! " Bobby jumped in gleefully.

Matthew couldn't see anything funny about it. " You shut up," he told his brother with a truculent scowl.

" I don't like the expression ' shut up,' " Claudia observed.

" He says it all the time," Bobby told her virtuously. " He's got a lot of bad habits now."

Matthew changed the subject. " I want to go to camp," he announced.

Bobby grabbed his arm with suppressed vehemence.

" You're not supposed to worry mother about that yet," he hissed, " so you just better shut up."

" Bobby said ' shut up,' " Matthew promptly pointed out.

It was a vicious circle, into which Claudia felt that she must break sooner or later. " Now listen, both of you, shut up ! " she commanded with finality.

After a moment's startled silence they knew that it was all right to laugh. Bertha came in horrified at all the noise, but too full up about the baby to do more than make a perfunctory gesture to quiet them down. " How do bees bring a baby ? " Matthew queried suddenly.

" You've got it mixed up, you dope," said Bobby.

" We go now," said Bertha. " Mamma is tired."

" No, I'm not tired," Claudia denied. However, she didn't have the energy to go into the bee business—— Matthew was too apt to follow an idea through to its bitter end, and bees would only leave him up in the air. " What was that you said about camp, Matthew ? " she reverted, to take his mind off.

" I want to go," Matthew replied succinctly.

Bertha gave him a reproachful look. " Mr. Naughton told them not to bother you about it."

" He said to wait until you came home," Bobby inter-polated, " and then you'd say ' yes '—maybe," he qualified with a prick of honesty.

" Maybe," Claudia echoed dryly. The question of camp had come up a couple of months ago, and she had said, " Definitely no." Now she could see exactly what had hap-pened—the children had made hay in her absence, and although David wasn't a groupist by a long shot, he wasn't above wanting his sons to swim and ride and take care of themselves in the woods, just like any other father. It was only mothers, she reflected gloomily, that would rather have a live sissy than a dead athlete.

She had every reason to believe that Bertha would think along the same lines, and throw her considerable weight toward postponing the issue for another year or two. It was disconcerting, therefore, to discover that she could not count on Bertha as an ally when the subject came up again the evening after she came home from the hospital. " The city is no place for children in the summer time," Bertha declared. " If we had the farm, it would be different."

" We can always rent," Claudia argued. " It won't cost very much more to rent a little cottage nearby somewhere,

where Mr. David could come out every night and get the air, too."

"Mr. David does not care to go out every night to get air," David lowered his newspaper to remark. "Also, Dr. Rowland says you're to have a complete rest from a big household this summer."

"Then I'm at the bottom of this. I'm supposed to take it easy, so we're to throw two-thirds of the children willy-nilly into camp."

"Exactly," said David, "and with the exception of one newly-born baby, presto, we're back in our honeymoon days."

"That part of it sounds very alluring," Claudia admitted, "but we'd still be running an expensive household, if not a big one. I mean——" she hesitated, not wanting to remind David in Bertha's presence, that a staff of two was more than they could afford with the boys away. She didn't have to finish, though. Bertha looked at David, and David nodded, and Bertha took up eagerly, "That is one of the reasons, too."

"One of what reasons, too?"

"I think Mary misses Katie, they were so used to working together all these years. Anyway, Mary told me that after you were well again, she would like to take a different kind of position. Her brother runs a bakery shop. She would like to serve in the store."

"Oh," said Claudia. She was probably not as strong as she thought she was, for the prospect of three children and twelve rooms and no Mary was a little appalling.

"It is not easy these days," Bertha continued, "to get anybody else."

"I don't doubt it," said Claudia faintly. "I wouldn't take this position myself, these days or any days."

"But if the children go to camp," Bertha pointed out, "we do not need anybody in Mary's place. I can easily do the little bit of work for you and Mr. David."

"And take care of the baby too? What do you think you're made of?"

"All right, we have a cleaning woman once in a while," Bertha threw in magnanimously. "And on hot nights you can drive out to the country for supper, and maybe go away weekends with Mr. David."

"I must say I'm very tempted," Claudia murmured to David. "Are you sure it'll be all right to let the children go?"

" I'll write you a written guarantee," said David.

She was a fool to believe him, but she did. It was like resting the whole burden of responsibility upon his shoulders. She had a sudden awareness that it wasn't right to depend on anyone as she depended on David. It wasn't so different from the way that Julia felt about " V."

ELEVEN

IMMEDIATELY, beginning the next morning, the whole household became camp-minded. They ate and slept and breathed camp. Bobby appointed himself major-domo of the project. "The first thing you have to do," he instructed, "is to order name-tapes. Everybody has to have name-tapes."

"You don't say," said Claudia. "Suppose you just mind your own little business and let Bertha and me manage things."

Name-tapes, however, proved a necessary evil and as soon as they arrived, Bertha put Claudia to sewing them on. She hotly resented the assignment. It was like giving Matthew peas to shell to keep him out of mischief. She was supposed to stay off her feet, and the name-tapes certainly saw to it that she did.

"I never did like to sew," she grumbled to David one evening, as she finished the last of a stack of handkerchiefs. "Just look at my finger, will you? There's an absolute hole in it."

"Why don't you wear a thimble?" David asked, without raising his eyes from the blueprint he was studying.

"I do wear one," she said, "but I don't push the needle with the finger I wear it on."

"Why not?" asked David.

"I always haven't," said Claudia.

Bobby came in before he went to bed to check up on her progress. The inordinate interest that he showed in his wardrobe would have been something to worry about if he weren't David's son. "You have to do every sock, too," he reminded her.

"I am cognizant of that delightful fact. And let me tell you," she went on with rising ire, "I wouldn't go through this again for my best friend. I expect you to be grateful for as long as you live, and take care of me in my old age to boot."

He grinned, but immediately his face froze in apprehension when he saw that she was tagging his brown sweater.

"What's that?" he demanded hoarsely.

"What does it look like?" She bit the thread off, and folded the sweater, ready to pack. His hand reached out.

" But I can't use my old one," he bleated. " I have to have a blue one."

" The list said ' one heavy sweater.' " Claudia maintained, " and this is one heavy sweater."

" But it has to be blue," he sought to impress upon her. " You have to buy it extra, all the boys have blue ones ! "

" That's silly," said Claudia flatly. " A sweater's a sweater."

She could see his normal affection change into an inimical remoteness. They were as far apart as the poles. " It has to be blue," he insisted in numb despair. " It has to be blue."

" You sound like an old song record. One more word and you'll sew these nasty little things on yourself. That'll fix you."

She expected him to grin again, but instead tragedy settled upon his lips. She put her arms around him. This was the very time, with David sitting across the room, to play the role of wise and loving mother. " Darling," she said beautifully, " you must look on this as a little exercise in character building. Isn't it enough that Dad is spending a lot of money sending you and Matthew to camp ? Is it necessary for you to have exactly what all the other fellows have ? Surely you can be above that kind of petty rivalry."

He didn't know what " petty rivalry " meant, but he took a chance, and said doggedly that it wasn't petty rivalry, he just wanted a blue sweater.

" We can't have everything we want in this life," Claudia told him with a simple, quiet finality. " Now good night, dear."

" Good night," he said.

" No kiss ? "

He placed an empty peck upon her cheek.

" Good night, Bobby," David said.

" Good night, Dad," said Bobby.

David waited until he was out of the room. " I hope you had a nice time listening to yourself," he remarked pleasantly.

Matthew wandered in before she could rally her dignity. " Button your pyjamas," she said mechanically.

" I am," said Matthew. He deposited a sloppy kiss upon her lips—Matthew liked to kiss. He said, " How many more weeks before we go to camp ? "

" You can count." said David.

" Three," said Matthew.

" Two," Claudia contradicted. " This one is practically

over. Matthew, I have a nice surprise for you. How would you like to wear Bobby's best brown sweater to camp? Instead of a new blue one, I mean. You can have your choice."

"Bobby's," Matthew decided promptly, and added swiftly, "Does he know?"

"Not yet," said Claudia.

Matthew licked his chops. "He'll be mad," he offered with gratification. "He'll be mad as anything."

"It'll be good for his character," said Claudia. "Go call him."

Matthew did not need to be coaxed. He raised his voice. "Bobby!" he shouted. "Mother wants you! She wants you right away!"

"Hush, you'll wake the baby," Claudia reproved him.

"Go deliver the message," David interjected. "What sort of manners is yelling?"

Bobby appeared at the door, armed with a scowl. Claudia scowled, too. "Bobby," she forestalled him severely. "I don't want any arguments, you're to be a nice generous boy and let your little brother have your brown sweater for camp."

Bobby's tragic mask cracked into a broad smirk. "Do I have to?" he whimpered, and then gave in at once with such elaborate reluctance that Matthew began to get sceptical. "Bobby can keep it," he said.

"Nonsense, your brother has to learn not to be selfish," Claudia determined. Complacently she ripped Bobby's name from the brown sweater, and sewed on Matthew's name instead. She caught David's eyebrow climbing up his forehead, and blew him a kiss. Men made better fathers than women, but women were better managers.

Before she knew it, June was upon them, and almost finished with, and the children left for camp in a sweltering blaze of heat. "I'm so grateful they're getting out of the city," Claudia asserted above a heavy heart, as they drove down to the station in a taxi. She glanced at David. "I only wish you could get off into the country, too. This weather seems to get you down."

She wondered whether it was the heat that gave him that waxy look around the ears. She wanted to say, "I don't like the way your ears look," but there was no rhyme or reason to the way she felt. She was smart enough to know that if she did not exercise the utmost vigilance, all her fears would be flooding back on her in full force. The children going away was probably the trigger that was starting her off again. Greedily, she wanted to encompass the four of them just as they were at this moment and hold them forever unchanged. The baby, oddly, stood outside her fears. He had not yet become a part of their close oneness, he seemed rather to belong to Bertha—a loan to fill the void that Fritz's death had left. " The trouble is, you feel so detached from a bottle baby," Claudia had mourned to David.

" Be a sport and give the first two a break, too," he had suggested blandly. And she had thought how right, how terribly right he was, and she had made up her mind then and there not to worry about them when they went to camp.

Her courage wavered, however, when she met their respective councillors at the train. " They don't look in the least like Harvard graduates," she whispered to David in dismay.

" What do Harvard graduates look like ? " David whispered back. Claudia said she didn't know, and David told her that, as it happened, they looked exactly like Harvard graduates. " Oh, dear," said Claudia, " neither of them will ever know what's what with a child."

" It's high time," said David, " that Matthew and Bobby knew what was what themselves. Besides, there's a camp physician."

" He's in the catalogue," said Claudia, peering around, " but I don't see a sign of him at the station."

" Stop worrying," David commanded.

" I am," she said meekly.

At the last minute, Bobby's arms tightened around her neck for a convulsive instant. " Don't go off to Iceland without us," he gulped with a watery smile. " Promise."

" I promise," said Claudia unsteadily. " We'll be meeting you right on this same spot two months from now when you come back."

" I want to stay home," Matthew announced abruptly, with his chin quivering.

" Not a chance," said David, " after your mother's sewed on all those name-tapes."

The crowded station became a vast desert of emptiness after they disappeared down the ramp. David steered her toward the street. " Walk to the office with me," he said, " the walk will do us both good."

At the entrance, he said, " Come on up, if you wait around a bit, we'll have lunch together."

" I can't. I have some shopping."

Much as she wanted the comfort of being with him, she was glad that she had invented an excuse, because he looked so relieved that she had things to do on her own. He kissed her. "All right, darling, I'll phone you later. Good-bye."

"Good-bye," she said.

She watched him disappear through the revolving door of the building, and her thoughts followed him up to his desk and the absorbing details of his work-filled day. Work was not only a great fulfilment, she realized suddenly, but it was probably one of the most important things in life. The question that Julia had asked her in the hospital—and to which she had replied so glibly—came back to her. Did she really have any qualms in giving up a possible stage career? Certainly she had never regretted it even now, although a job of any kind was what she needed this particular summer morning.

She felt desperately at loose ends, and yet she had a strange sense that this was only an interlude. It would avail her nothing to begin to run around like a chicken with its head cut of, in search of something to occupy herself. "A fine rationalization for laziness," she decided, as she hailed an uptown bus.

Somebody got out, which left an empty seat by the window. She slipped into it gratefully. Life was like that, on a large and complicated scale. Or was it? The bus was equally full of people who didn't get seats next to the window. "Maybe they don't want to sit by the window," she concluded. It was a surprisingly simple answer to all the unfairness in the world.

It was funny that her mind should suddenly start to move in thoughts. She probably did as much thinking as anybody else, but not so that it was noticeable. A great deal of otherwise conscious contemplation seemed to be taken up in the blind faith that everything happened for a reason, and in her particular case—for the best reason. She made a grimace at herself—she was the image of the little hairdresser in Eastbrook who used to keep small pamphlets on astrology and Unity in the drawer of her manicuring table. People had to live by something, though, and it didn't make much difference what that something was as long as it took a general upward direction.

"The trouble with me is," Claudia reflected, "that I've been borrowing bits and pieces of everybody else's philosophy, instead of finding one of my own." For example, she had been perfectly willing to believe that selling the farm and using Elizabeth's apartment was a fortuitous marking of time until some momentous change took place in their lives. Secretly, she was beginning to doubt that that change was coming. For all of Julia's messages from the other world, the Iceland commission was no nearer a decision than it had been six months ago. Labour conditions and slow production might easily hold the project up for another year or two, and she was fast getting to the point where she was ready to call the whole deal off as a bad guess, and begin from scratch again. It was all very well to use Elizabeth's home as a temporary haven, but neither she nor David was the sort of person who liked the feeling of being in storage indefinitely. It wasn't good for the children either.

She was more than ever aware of a sense of not belonging as she let herself into the dim, spacious lounge of the apartment, now silent as a tomb. Bertha had lowered all the shades against the hot sun, and the doors of the boys' rooms were shut—closed for the summer—with Bertha's customary efficiency and dispatch.

She wandered through the long corridors, and finally found the baby on the terrace in his carriage with Bertha bending over him, full of applause and delight because he had finished every drop of his bottle. "Never was such a good baby," she greeted Claudia fervently. "Never."

"I'm glad you're pleased," said Claudia. She looked down at him. He was already asleep, and for the moment, exquisitely fragrant and sweet. "I think he's going to be pretty after all," she acknowledged.

"He is beautiful ! " Bertha declared indignantly.

"Very well," said Claudia, "have it your own way."

"I must get to my laundry," said Bertha happily. She turned at the threshold in sudden contrition. "It is lonesome for you," she said.

"A little," Claudia confessed. "I'll get used to it, though."

Bertha's eyes gave a little sigh. "You have your husband," she said. "That is the thing that counts the most."

"Yes," said Claudia. She knew it with her soul, but Bertha knew it with her body and her mind. Losing Fritz had meant the end of living, as Bertha knew it—emptiness beyond belief. Now Bertha was filling the emptiness, she was building a new life. It seemed right and fitting that the baby should help her over the first few months of loneliness and grief. "Also another fine rationalization for not taking care of my own child," Claudia amended inwardly.

" You and Mr. David should have a nice time this summer," Bertha went on. " You should forget you have children."

" Mr. David's pretty tired for any gallivanting."

" It will be the best thing for him," Bertha said.

David must have also felt that it was a good time to recapture their lost youth, for he telephoned at five o'clock. He said, " I'll be through at about seven, let's go out for dinner and make a night of it."

Her immediate impulse was to reply that they would eat at home, since she knew that Bertha had made chicken croquettes from yesterday's roast of veal, but economy seemed out of order. " Lovely," she agreed. " I'll be ready."

He had chosen for the occasion a horribly expensive restaurant off Madison Avenue, where he had had to use Julia's name to get a table—which was no small blow to his pride. " I don't blame you," Claudia sympathized. " This is not only snobbism, it's robbery. You'd think they'd at least put a potato on the plate, just for the looks of it."

" Order some potatoes," said David.

" I don't want any anyway, it's just the principle of the thing," she said.

Afterwards they went to a musical comedy, which was another form of robbery, six something apiece for highly inferior nonsense. But the following evening they really had a good time, for they had supper at home and went to an early movie around the corner. It wasn't at all crowded, but in line with David's usual luck, a woman chose to sit right in front of him, and most effectively blocked his vision. With unwonted courage he leaned forward and asked her to take her hat off. She turned around and gave him a frigid stare, and then he saw that she didn't have a hat on at all, it was her own hair that was sticking up in the air.

Immediately, Claudia got the hiccoughs. The woman said, " th, th," very loudly, and moved to another row in a huff. " Thank you," said Claudia. " Now if we only don't have a travel picture, everything will be perfect."

The air outside was sharply warm after the chilled theatre. David coughed a little. They bought some pastilles at the drugstore. " That air-conditioning makes my throat dry," he explained. " No more movies," Claudia decided to herself.

The apartment was blessedly cool. A river breeze came in

through the bedroom windows. " The baby's room is lovely, too," Claudia reported. " We might like staying home hereafter."

David grinned. " I guess we've paid our respects to youth." He flung himself across the wide expanse of the old Chippendale bed, and pulled her down beside him. They could have stayed there forever ; it was a nuisance to get undressed. " When we give up this apartment, I'm going to miss this bed," said Claudia.

" So am I," said David. " Let's buy another like it."

" Let's," said Claudia. " Twin beds are a waste of sheets." Their lips met. " Your face is awfully warm," she whispered.

" Why shouldn't it be ? " he whispered back.

" I hate to tell you but you're going to have company for dinner for the rest of the week," she informed Bertha the next morning."

" That's good, who ? " said Bertha cheerfully.

" Us," said Claudia. " We're going to pretend that Bobby and Matthew haven't gone to camp and so we don't have to have a second honeymoon."

Bertha didn't quite follow the line of reasoning, but her mind leapt immediately to a pot roast. " And I don't charge you extra for the potatoes," she promised.

Candy dropped in late that afternoon while Claudia was giving the baby a bath, and feeling very clumsy about it. " Bertha's making dumpling on pins and needles," Claudia explained. " She doesn't trust me. I don't trust myself, when he squirms and splashes like this. Watch out or you'll get all wet."

" Can I finish him up ? " Candy begged.

" With pleasure," said Claudia. " What brings you in town on such a warm day ? I should think Greenwich would be a great deal pleasanter place than the city."

" It isn't," said Candy briefly. " Anyway, I came in to buy John a birthday present."

Claudia smiled, thinking how birthdays had became less and less important through the years. It would shock Candy if she said so, though. " What did you get John ? " she asked.

" A ship's clock. His mother's given him a new boat. It's a thirty-two foot sloop, and sleeps four."

" Oh," said Claudia, somewhat awed. She had heard of

mothers giving sons shirts and neckties and wrist watches, but never thirty-two foot boats.

Candy lifted the baby onto the canvas dressing-table. "One good thing about it," she said, "we can get away weekends."

"Oh," said Claudia again. She could think of nothing that she would like less than going away weekends on a boat.

"You haven't met John's mother yet, have you?" Candy continued carefully.

"David and I were talking about it the other night," said Claudia. "She was ill the day of your wedding, and then the baby came and everything."

"I know. John wants you to come out for next Sunday dinner. The boat'll be in the water for the first time, and he wants you to see it." She glanced at her watch. "I telephoned him that I'd be here and he said he'd drive David home and pick me up."

"Good," said Claudia. "Why don't you both stay for dinner?"

"I'd love nothing better," said Candy. "Bertha makes the most wonderful smells when she cooks—it's the first time I've felt hungry in ages."

"Why?" Claudia asked bluntly.

Candy shrugged. "I don't know, I just haven't. Mother Payne gets furious. Not outwardly, of course. But I can tell."

"She probably worries about you as if you were her own daughter."

"Probably," said Candy. She turned the baby over and patted a drift of powder across his dimpled shoulders. "Is there anything more wonderful than a baby's fat little back?"

"His fat little legs and his fat little stomach," said Claudia.

Bertha appeared with his bottle wrapped in a napkin. "Thank you very much," she said, taking over.

A few minutes later John and David came. David pulled the little tail of hair that sprang with such audacious young sweetness from the back of Candy's head. "You here again," he said with affection if not tact.

"My wife seems to forget that she doesn't live at this address any longer," John commented lightly as he kissed her.

"I'm always that way where there's a baby," Candy was swift to explain. "Claudia can tell you how I was when Matthew was little."

"She was," Claudia nodded. "Even worse."

"She was five years younger then," John put his arm

around Candy's shoulders and tilted her face for a kiss. "You're a big girl now. You're married, with a home of your own. Remember ? "

He left himself wide open for a reply that Claudia hoped, tensely, Candy would refrain from making. But it was all too clear that Candy was young and unhappy and confused. " It's not a home of my own," she said.

John flushed a little. He started to say something, and then thought better of it. He picked up Candy's summer wrap and held it for her. " We'd better be going. Mother has guests for dinner, and we'll have to dress."

Candy took the coat instead of letting him put it across her shoulders. " Why can't we stay here ? I don't even know these friends of your mother's. Claudia's already asked us."

" It's a good idea," David chimed in. " While you girls talk, John and I can get some work done. What about it, John, we can go over the Anderson bid and be ready for him in the morning."

" I'd like to." He turned to Candy. " Did you let Mother know we mightn't come home ? "

" No, but we can call her."

John hesitated. He said, " I wouldn't then, dear, I'm afraid it's too late to upset her plans, she's counting on us."

" What's there to count on ? She won't be alone, she's having company."

" Exactly," said John. Claudia could see that he was determined to be casual. " Doesn't it occur to you that she might want to show off her new daughter-in-law ? "

" I doubt it," said Candy. She managed something that was meant to sound like a laugh. " I'm sure your mother thinks you should have married someone who'd be a much better wife than I am."

The flush on John's face deepened. " Now you're being a little silly," he said quietly.

Claudia could see the quick tears of chagrin and frustration spring to Candy's eyes. She had invited his rebuke, but the hurt was intolerable nonetheless. She could only hurt him back in defence. " That's apparently your mother's opinion, too," she replied in a choked voice.

For a long moment after they had gone, Claudia and David said nothing. " She should have her little tail kicked," David remarked at last, with less venom than compassion.

" John's tail could stand a kick, too," Claudia said. " It made me a little sick to hear them."

" Have you talked to Candy ? "

" No. I've been reading between the lines, but she hasn't said anything, so I didn't feel I ought to question her."

" I'm glad you didn't," said David. " If it's one thing I loathe it's women who go around inviting confidences and playing God."

She didn't tell him that she had had her lesson the time she'd held forth to Bobby on the little matter of sweaters and character building. " I can't imagine what's gone haywire," she said instead. " Candy was so fond of Mrs. Payne in the beginning."

" Two women in love with the same man," said David.

" Or vice versa," Claudia said.

Superficially, however, the Payne household harboured no dark shadows of involved relationships. " This is really awfully nice," Claudia commented, as their car turned in along a winding driveway of ancient maples the following Sunday. " What's Candy complaining about ? "

" Apparently not the scenery," David replied.

At first sight, there didn't seem to be anything to complain about in John's mother either. She looked like a very attractive little old lady, frail and white-haired, but Claudia almost fell over at the firmness of her handshake, and the full, unexpected vibrancy of her voice. After a half an hour of extremely stimulating conversation, during which Candy sat silent and depressed like a visitor in the house, it was not surprising to learn that Mrs. Payne had many talents. She could grow specimen plants, bind books, paint pictures, and sail a boat as well as any man. " Mother took our old Winddrift up to the Vineyard with Dad last year," John told them proudly.

" That's wonderful," said Claudia, who didn't know the first thing about boats.

" The sea is in our blood," Mrs. Payne enlarged, smilingly. " I come from a long line of shipbuilders, you see—I'm afraid, though, that that trip to the Vineyard was my last sail. Candy will have to take my place hereafter."

" The doctor says that Mother's got what's called a tired heart," John explained.

" I don't wonder it's tired," thought Claudia. Bobby and Matthew and the baby didn't know how lucky they were that she didn't have long lines of a single thing in her blood—it would leave the field so much clearer for their wives. " I will never," she vowed silently, " be a playmate to my sons. I'd rather be just a passing stranger who happened to give them birth."

David must have had much the same reaction, because the minute they got outside the gates driving home he said, " Pretty fatiguing, wasn't it ? "

" It's as good a word as any," said Claudia. " There's only one solution as far as I can see."

" What ? "

" Candy and John ought to be living in the apartment instead of us."

" I talked to John about that the day after they were over to see us. He says it's too large and expensive to keep up."

" It is, but it's better than nothing until they're able to find a small place of their own. Besides, expense shouldn't mean anything next to their happiness. Candy has loads of money."

" John won't touch it. That isn't his idea of building for happiness. And he's right."

" Sometimes it's more right to be wrong," said Claudia. " And this is one of the times."

David didn't say it was, and he didn't say it wasn't. " There's another reason," he went on, " John told me that his mother is sicker than even she thinks she is, and it would be a little tough on her if he walked out now."

" It's a little tough on his wife if he stays. A mother image can certainly mess up a marriage, can't it ? "

" Yes, it certainly can," David sombrely agreed.

" It might have even messed ours up if you and Mamma hadn't known what it was all about," said Claudia. " I still miss her frightfully," she broke off with honesty. " Is that normal ? "

" I miss her myself," said David.

Claudia sighed with satisfaction. " It's wonderful to have ten years of adjustment behind us. There's something so sad about youth stumbling along, making its mistakes."

" Yes, Grandma," David said. He put his free hand on her knee. " It was a nice day, anyway, wasn't it ? The country smelled so good, and the Sound looked so clear and blue."

" Yes, it was lovely. I hate the thought of your coming back in the grime and smoke of the city."

" What about you ? Am I any better than you are ? "

" You're in a stuffy office all day. You need sun and air more than I do."

" Well, let's have a little of it ourselves," he said. " John wants us to come out early next Saturday, and go off for the weekend with them."

She stared at him aghast. " In that tiny sailboat ?   All of us ? "

" It isn't tiny, it sleeps four very comfortably. She's a little beauty. Did you notice the teak decks and the stainless steel rigging ? "

" I did not," she told him crisply. She didn't like the sudden enthusiasm in his voice, nor the way his face lit up. " I hope you haven't got any old sea captains or shipbuilders lurking around in your blood, too," she said.

" I always liked boats," he admitted sheepishly.

She had an uneasy presentiment that a little extra bit of adjustment was looming up in the immediate future.

TWELVE

AT BREAKFAST the next morning she said, " I haven't a thing to wear on the boat, I think I'll go downtown and get some slacks. Aren't you going to finish your cereal ? "

" I've had enough," said David.

" I'm glad you think it's enough. A cup of coffee and half a piece of toast is nothing to do a day's work on."

" It's too hot to eat." He pushed his chair back. " Get your slacks tomorrow, you're going to Dr. Rowland's today."

" What for ? "

" Must we go into that again ? He wants to give you a final check up before he leaves for his vacation."

" I can't see the point of it."

" Never mind the point. Just do as you're told. I'll meet you at his office at twelve sharp."

" You don't have to go with me. Why lock the barn door after the horse is out ? "

" Your metaphors are highly unpoetical." He bent to kiss her. " If you're a good girl, I'll take you out to lunch afterwards. Good-bye." He was out of the door before she could find her tongue.

" This is the most ridiculous thing ! " she sputtered to Bertha, who had come in to clear the table. " I didn't have to be checked up three months after Bobby and Matthew."

" You don't remember," Bertha offered mildly. " Anyway, it is nothing to make a fuss about. If Mr. David wants you to go, you should go."

" Mr. David is a fine one to dictate to anyone else. Look at that breakfast—and all last night he tossed and turned——"

" It is the heat, maybe," Bertha said. " The air was very heavy, I did not sleep much either. I have your good slip and panties nicely ironed."

" I didn't say I was going," Claudia grumbled. Still, the thought of having lunch with David was an inducement. At least she'd see to it that he ate a decent meal instead of getting by with a sandwich and a bottle of buttermilk sent in to the office.

At eleven o'clock he telephoned to say that he couldn't get away because a client had just flown in from the coast.

" Sorry about lunch, darling. Call Dr. Rowland and make an appointment for tomorrow at the same time."

This was a nuisance. She was practically dressed and she had no intention of wasting the slip and panties. Also, there was no earthly reason for David to tag along with her. Dr. Rowland would merely go through his customary cut and dried procedure, and dismiss her until the next baby.

It turned out, though, that there wasn't ever going to be another baby. She was a fool not to have suspected it before, for apparently everyone knew it but herself. Even the receptionist seemed to know it. She gave Claudia an unusually pleasant smile as she ushered her into the waiting-room, and said that Doctor would try to squeeze her in immediately. It was an unheard of privilege to be able to squeeze in immediately at Dr. Rowland's. His office was always full of patients no matter how far ahead of time she got there, and she had decided as far back as the end of Bobby that there was no use trying to be the first. It was one of the minor mysteries of an obstetrician's practice.

This morning was no exception to the rule. Indeed, the war seemed to have speeded things up, both before and after, for every chair was filled. She had to perch on a narrow window seat, which nobody else would have been able to manage as well. She studied the roomful of women surreptitiously, and surreptitiously, they studied her, wondering whether she had just begun or just finished. She couldn't help feeling complacent. Dr. Rowland's clientele might be one of the wealthiest in the city, but she certainly looked more stylish than anyone else in the room, even in her inexpensive old print dress. Each and every one of the others was past the point where an expensive gown, or a string of pearls could do them a bit of good. They were all sisters under the skin.

She could feel their envious eyes upon her, as, far ahead of turn, the nurse beckoned her from the threshold, and she rose and moved gracefully into Dr. Rowland's private office.

" Well, well, well," he greeted her from behind his Sheraton desk. " You're looking very well, how do you feel ? Splendid, splendid ! Complete examination, Miss Darcy."

He made the complete examination, and then he sat down again behind his desk, and motioned her to sit down, too.

" Mrs. Naughton's chart, Miss Darcy."

" It's right in front of you, Doctor."

He drew it toward him. " And how's the baby coming along ? Thriving nicely ? "

"Very nicely," said Claudia.

"Splendid—now, let me see, your last visit to me was on—Miss Darcy, you've given me the wrong chart—you've given me Mrs. Hartley Naughton's chart."

Miss Darcy came rushing back from getting the examination room ready for the next patient. "Oh I'm so sorry, Doctor—Mrs. *David* Naughton, of course—here it is——"

Claudia's complacency deepened. There was a great difference in charts, for Julia had been steadily losing bits and pieces of her anatomy for the past ten years, and getting nothing in return but bills. "And how are the other two boys?" Dr. Rowland went on, as he studied the fruitful record in front of him.

"Fine," said Claudia. "They're at camp."

"Splendid, splendid," Dr. Rowland approved. "And your husband?"

Claudia hesitated. While Dr. Rowland was in this expansive mood, she might broach the subject of David's being a little run down and get his advice. "David isn't in too awfully good shape, I don't think," she started off tentatively——

"Splendid, splendid," Dr. Rowland interjected heartily, still scanning the chart. "And as for yourself—tell me about yourself—no undue fatigue, no sensation of pain or discomfort?"

"None."

Dr. Rowland made note of the fact with small, indecipherable scratches of his pen. "And you sleep well, and you eat well——"

"There's absolutely nothing wrong with me," Claudia broke in impatiently, although it was exceedingly nice of him to show his interest in her general condition, considering the fact that he took care of her at reduced rates. "I know I was a nuisance to you in the hospital," she went on apologetically. "I was probably out of practice. David and I are so anxious for a daughter, though, that it won't be five years until next time, I'm sure of that."

It was then that Dr. Rowland told her that there wasn't going to be a next time. "We can't let you take that chance again," he finished up solemnly. "It was nothing short of a miracle that we were able to save both you and the child."

She was stunned. "Does David know? I mean that we can't have any more children? That we can't have a daughter, I mean?"

" He knew the night the baby was born."

" That's why he wanted to come with me," her mind groped.
" That's why I was supposed to take it easy for a few
months——"

" However, there is nothing at all to worry about now,"
Dr. Rowland assured her. " Sometimes these things leave ill
effects—very often the condition requires surgical interference
—but in your case, I'm happy to say, we need anticipate no
trouble. In fact, I dismiss you as a patient." He rose from
the desk, reached for her hand and pumped it cordially,
pushing her out at the same time. It was a trick, peculiarly
his own, during busy office hours.

The waiting-room was more crowded than ever. Claudia
hurried blindly past it, her eyes filled with tears, and her heart
no longer complacent.

She didn't want David to know how she felt about not
having another baby, but when he came home that evening,
she began to cry like a fool. " Don't mind me," she gulped,
" I'm just being maudlin. I mean, after all, I have three
children already, why should I feel like this ? "

" It's a funny thing, why," said David soberly, " but it does
hit hard."

" When I had the miscarriage, it hit hard too. It must touch
something very fundamental in a woman's makeup."

" It does," said David.

" The main reason is that I've let you down. I promised
you a girl, and now you'll never have one."

" I wouldn't know what to say to a girl." He put his arms
around her. " Look, darling, the main reason isn't that you've
let me down, it's that you've let yourself down. It's a question
of pride, basically. It riles the life out of you to have to buckle
down to any limitations. If you want a dozen babies, you
want to be able to have them, and no back talk from your
insides."

" Maybe."

" No ' maybe ' about it."

" I'm not ready to admit it. All I know is I wanted a
daughter, and I wanted you to have a daughter."

" I'm perfectly willing to call quits on three sons. Suppose
I'd been married to Julia ? I wouldn't even have had
a dog."

" Poor Julia. I'm never going to make fun of her any more.
And poor Edith Dexter. Losing her only child and never

5

being able to have another one. All at once, I feel so sorry for all the women I used to look down on."

"It's what is generally called growing mellow with age," said David.

"I wonder if it isn't," said Claudia reflectively. "I remember when Mamma died, that suddenly I was terribly conscious of all the people who had lost their mothers, or who were going to lose them. And your being in the war, and my having a miscarriage—and even my appendix—made me feel more in touch with the things that keep happening to people."

"At that rate," said David, half in jest, "if you live long enough, you'll be a very live person."

She made a little face. "Thank you, but I'd just as soon not be."

"Nobody's going to ask you," he said. "You'll take what you get and like it."

"I'll take it," she said, "but I don't guarantee to like it."

It was odd how the small philosophy, so newly born within her, applied to the most trivial and unlikely experiences. The boat, for example. She had never realized before that there were so many people who were boat-minded. Boats, to a vast section of humanity, were not only a form of pastime, they were an avocation, a religion. On Saturday of that same week she was plunged into a whole new world she had never known existed. It began, actually, the day before. David, who never turned on the radio, turned it on at breakfast, and listened to the weather report.

"It's hot and humid, I can tell you that without listening," said Claudia, who didn't like to hear about soapsuds while she drank her coffee.

"I want to hear what it says about tomorrow."

"Oh, are we still going out sailing with John and Candy ? "

"Yes, of course. They expect us. Don't you want to ? "

"I didn't know whether you wanted to," she hedged.

"I've been looking forward to it."

"So have I," she said, with a wrinkling of her nose that he didn't see.

He was up before seven the next morning. "I don't know what the great rush is about," Claudia demurred. "We have all weekend."

"The best time to get under way, if you're going any place," David enlightened her, "is at dawn."

"It doesn't sound particularly relaxing. Where are we going that we have to get there so passionately?"

"Some nice little harbour over on Long Island. Next time, we can get an early start and go a little farther."

"Long Island sounds far enough to me. Will I be able to phone home?"

"Probably not. Why should you?"

"Suppose something went wrong with the baby."

"It won't. You couldn't get back in a hurry, anyway."

"That makes me feel fine."

To add to her tribulations, letters came from Bobby and Matthew just as they were leaving. She read them in the car. Matthew wrote, in gigantic print, "I CAN RIDE HORSE-BACK NOW," and Bobby wrote in a drunken scrawl with flourishes, "We are going on a canoe trip and my shooting teacher says I am very good with a gun, and I am one of the best divers, your loving son, Bobby."

Claudia swallowed her discomfiture. She was ashamed to let David see that Bobby's glib recital of his accomplishments sent chills of foreboding down her spine. David, however, must have been a little discomfited himself because he said, "Stop worrying, they're all right, they're fine." He reached for the radio dial, and kept turning it back and forth, with a great deal of static, until he got the weather: Rising winds. Small craft warnings from Hatteras to Cape May.

"It sounds bad," Claudia offered hopefully. "I guess we mightn't go after all."

"Nonsense," said David. "Of course we'll go."

"But aren't we small craft?"

"You sound as if you were scared."

"Don't be silly."

"We're not going anywhere near Cape May," he assured her. He turned the radio off, and put his hand on her knee and kept it there in sheer good-will. She resisted the impulse to remind him that it was safer to drive with both hands on the wheel. She couldn't get over how he seemed really to be looking forward to this sail. She hoped, devoutly, that she would not disgrace him by getting seasick. True, she had never been seasick in her life, but then she hadn't been on boats very often—infrequently on ferries, and only once on an ocean steamer when she was young. "Does it get very rough?" she asked him with a hypocritical air of wanting it to be rough.

"You bet it can get rough," he replied with satisfaction.

" What fun," she murmured.

Candy and John were already on the boat when they got down to the dock. They were barefooted and wore practically nothing. Claudia had bought a good-looking pair of slacks, but Candy told her to put on a bathing suit instead, she'd be soaked in no time. " How ? " said Claudia.

" I don't know what you mean, ' how,' " Candy answered. " You just will."

" Oh," said Claudia.

She found it somewhat difficult to accommodate herself not only to the cramped quarters below deck, but to the subtle weaving of the floor beneath her feet. She was glad to get up into the air again. " You look awfully cute," Candy appraised her, " not a bit like the mother of three children. Isn't it going to be just perfect ? "

" I hope so," said Claudia.

The deck was slippery. " Hey ! " David expostulated, and caught her just in time. " You'd better sit down," he advised her kindly, " until we get under way."

She sat down. In a little while they were under way, with John and David working like lunatics, shouting to each other as they pulled up anchor and threw ropes and hoisted sails. " I never knew David knew so much about boats," Candy said in surprise.

" Neither did I," said Claudia. " It just never came up, because we've never lived near the water, I suppose."

" He's almost as good as John," Candy complimented her. " I love being married to an athletic man, don't you ? "

" Within reason," said Claudia guardedly. " What's this ' gibsle ' they're yelling about ? "

" The little sail," said Candy.

" Oh, so that's the way you pronounce it," said Claudia. The boat dipped over on its side, and lurched into the air and down. She clutched the rail and closed her eyes, pretty sure that they were never going to come up again.

" Isn't this great ! " David shouted in her ear. She nodded feebly. Apparently you always went down, and you always came up.

She counted the hours. There were five of them, one worse than another, before they dropped anchor in a still blue harbour dotted with other sail boats. Slowly, painfully, little knots all over her body began to untie themselves. She went below deck, where Candy was busy opening a can of baked beans.

How could Candy be so blithe about it ? She wanted to help, but she didn't feel like it. " Why beans ? " she bleated.

" It's always beans," said Candy. " John says they stick to your ribs better than anything else on a boat."

" It's not my ribs I'm worried about," said Claudia.

Candy stared at her. " You weren't seasick, were you ? "

Claudia managed a small laugh. " Good Heavens, no ! " she said. " I think David would disown me if I were that kind of a woman."

Candy giggled. " We all would," she said.

" Now you see what you're up against," Claudia told herself grimly.

By exercising the most rigid control, she tackled her beans. To her complete amazement, they tasted good beyond belief. It seemed impossible that they were only beans. David ate three platefuls of them. " We'll dig some clams for supper, then you'll see what good food really is. This is great, isn't it ? " he repeated like a chant.

" Yes," Claudia admitted, " it is." She thanked her lucky stars that she had got over the worst of it without his knowing how great it hadn't been.

After lunch, they lay out on deck, and then took a swim off the side of the boat. The water was icy cold, and there were jelly fish. " They won't hurt you ! " Candy shouted. " Just dive in ! It's glorious ! "

Claudia stepped gingerly down the ladder, and while no one was looking, stepped back up again. After all, she was the only one of them who'd just had a baby, and couldn't have another.

Toward twilight, a number of cruisers came chugging into the harbour. It was as if a very objectionable odour had suddenly invaded the sweetness of the air. " We'll have to shove off to the Cove," said John, with his nose up.

" Right," said David.

" What's wrong ? " Claudia asked. " I thought this was so great."

" Sail boats don't like motor boats," Candy explained.

Halfway home the next day the wind suddenly died down and they were becalmed. Claudia was very pleased with the sudden respite. She hurried below deck, and ate a piece of fried chicken left over from lunch. John and David each had a highball and Candy did away with the last of the fruit. " This is nice after rollicking along on one ear," said Claudia.

"Not too nice," said Candy. "I hope the wind comes up soon."

"Why ? "

"So we can get home," said Candy simply.

"We've got a motor," said Claudia. "Doesn't it work ? "

"It works, but we never use it. John would rather sit here all night than use the auxiliary."

"That's not normal," said Claudia. She went in search of David to talk some sense into him. She found him polishing brass, and perfectly happy. He wouldn't be found dead polishing brass at home, she reflected bitterly. "How long are we going to sit here ? " she asked with a degree of acid in her voice.

"Until the wind comes up," he replied cheerfully.

"And if it doesn't ? "

"It will."

It didn't. One of the passing cruisers, full of people and dish towels drying, offered to tow them.

"No, thank you ! " John and David called back in a single voice. The little motor boat tossed its flat backside, and in no time at all was out of sight, puffing busily along toward the Connecticut shore. "Why didn't they let them ? " Claudia muttered rebelliously to Candy.

"Too proud," said Candy briefly.

"Oh, shoot," said Claudia.

Eventually, because all things had to change sometimes, the wind stopped dying down and came up in a great to-do. John and David clapped each other on the shoulders, and behaved as if they, personally, had caused it to blow. "Put a man on a boat and he becomes an idiot," Claudia decided.

Bertha was worried because they got home so late. "I thought you were drowned," she greeted them.

"I thought so, too," said Claudia. "How's the baby ? Any messages ? "

"Fine," said Bertha. "Miss Julia telephoned, but nothing special. And also Mrs. Riddle. She said Mr. David should call her as soon as he comes in."

"Watch me," David jeered. "I'm going to soak in a hot tub."

Bertha looked after him as if she could not believe her eyes. "But he is so sunburned ! Like a different man after two days only."

"Isn't he ? " Claudia exulted. "And you should have seen what he ate for breakfast this morning. Banana and cereal and two eggs and piles of toast."

" You are joking," said Bertha flatly.

" I'm not, I think he would have eaten three eggs with a little encouragement."

" Then you should go out on the boat every weekend," Bertha ordained.

" We are," said Claudia.   Her feelings about it were mixed.

THIRTEEN

AS THE SUMMER wore on, she discovered that you could get used to anything—even boats. She wrote bragging letters to the children, matching their feats with her own, and David enlarged most generously upon her achievements. "You ought to see the big fish Mamma caught," he'd add in a postscript. Or, "When you boys see your Mamma handle a sail, you'll look to your laurels."

"They won't know what 'looking to laurels' means," Claudia protestedly modestly.

The best part of the whole summer, however, was watching David grow browner and browner—almost leathery with the sun and wind—although she couldn't understand why he didn't gain an ounce, in spite of all the beans and cereal and toast which he continued to stow away in huge quantities.

"John doesn't put on any weight either," Candy consoled her, as they were lying on the forward deck one Sunday afternoon in late August. "He's much skinnier than David is, too."

"I'm much what than David ? " John called over.

"Handsomer, nicer, and more remarkable ! " Candy called back with a kiss.

"I like that," said David. There was no occasion for scintillating repartee, but nevertheless there was a heaviness in his voice that made Claudia sit up. "You're both wearing yourselves out cleaning those heavy anchors," she scolded. "They're clean enough, why don't you come over here and rest ! "

"We're almost through," said David.

Candy lay back again, stretching luxuriously. "Leave them alone, they don't think it's work, they enjoy it."

"They're dripping with sweat."

"It's much better than not sweating," said Candy. "All the poisons or something come out."

"Those anchors must weigh a ton."

"They are terribly heavy," Candy agreed. "John's got another kind on order. They're made of some new metal, very light. They ought to be here any day now."

"I hope so. I hate seeing them toss that much weight around, you'd think they'd burst a blood vessel."

"Lie back and relax," said Candy comfortably. "They know enough not to hurt themselves."

Claudia leaned on her elbow, looking down at Candy. "You don't worry about John at all, do you?" she remarked with a kind of wonder.

"No," said Candy, and added, without guile, "Should I?"

"You should not," said Claudia. "Men don't like to be worried about." She shielded her eyes from the hot sun, and stared out at the sheet of blue water, spread across the earth like a fancy cloth of sequins. "I wish I didn't. It's my besetting sin."

"I don't think I know enough to worry," Candy admitted honestly. "John had a little infection inside his nostril a couple of weeks ago. I didn't think anything of it, but his mother called the doctor, and the doctor said he could have died of it, if it had been neglected. I just didn't worry because I didn't realize what it meant, I suppose. I mean, I don't deserve any credit for it."

"I wasn't giving you credit," said Claudia. "I was envying you."

"It doesn't mean I'm not in love with John. I think I'd die if anything ever happened to him. I couldn't go on living."

"I'm afraid you'd have to," said Claudia.

"I wouldn't want to."

"That's another story."

"This summer's been so wonderful for us," Candy continued tremulously. "It's brought us so much closer." She faltered a little. "Not that we weren't——"

"I know," said Claudia softly.

"He's a different person when he's away from his family."

"Most people are."

"I'll try never to tie my children," Candy vowed.

"I try, but I don't succeed too well."

"You were very good about letting them go to camp. After all, Matthew's hardly more than a baby."

"I wouldn't have had the courage if it hadn't been for David."

"They'll be home soon, won't they?"

"Day after tomorrow. I can't wait to see them."

"I don't blame you. The summer went fast, didn't it?"

"Very. Now that I look back on it."

They fell into a friendly silence, broken only by the soft lapping of water against the sides of the boat. John tiptoed up behind them, and scared Candy into a small shriek. She didn't have to shriek but she seemed to want to. They were like puppies playing together, Claudia thought.

She looked around for David. " He went below to wash up," John answered her unspoken question. " What have you two girls been gabbling about at the rate of a mile a minute ? "

" Don't you wish you knew," said Candy teasingly.

John's left eyebrow slid up his forehead in a way he'd borrowed from David without knowing it. He reached for one of her taffy-coloured braids, but she was too swift for him, and a moment later they were overboard with a great splash, and chasing each other as if they were on dry land. Claudia watched them, tolerant and amused. It was a long while since she and David had gone in for such sweet, wild antics. Perhaps as one grew older there was less need of that kind of emotional release. Yet watching them filled her with a desire to be near him. She wondered what was keeping him so long.

He wasn't in the galley or the cabin or the cockpit, and on a boat there was only a limited number of places you could go. She heard him cough—something, but not quite like the little cough he always blamed on smoking. " David ! " she called, and added, superfluously. " Where are you ? "

There was no answer. She tried the door. It wasn't locked so quite naturally she opened it and walked in. He was standing at the basin with his back to her, and then he turned the tap on, but not quite quickly enough. It happened so fast that she wasn't even frightened, for her brain, in mercy, refused the impact of her eyes. She just stood there, frozen, wondering if she had really seen what she'd thought she'd seen. " David——" she whispered at last, " what was that ? "

For as long as she lived, she would never forget the strange colour that whiteness made beneath his sunburn, nor the way his lips tugged sideways in the semblance of a grin. " It looked," he said, " like an awful lot of red ink."

The trip home took interminable hours, though a fresh wind pushed them steadily along. David gave over the tiller to Candy. " Here, lazy," he said, " you do a little work for a change." He sat quietly in the cockpit, holding his pipe in his mouth but not lighting it. Claudia sat next to him, very quietly. " What's the matter with you two ? " John demanded. " You're acting like company."

" We had a fight," Claudia explained. " We're sulking."

"Oh yes, I believe that," Candy hooted. "No, but is anything the matter really?"

"Just sulking," David insisted.

It was odd how, with one accord, they said nothing of what had happened. Candy and John were at the beginning of their love, building its foundation on small joys and smaller griefs; they had the capacity to understand, but not the experience to encompass. Claudia was glad that the business of sailing kept them occupied. Mute with terror, she kept straining to see the opposite shore. The sun was going down, and the sea no longer danced and shimmered. It was growing sullen and unfriendly. If only, she prayed, it would not conspire against them with its eternally changing moods. Her eyes sought David's.

"Cheer up," he said, "we're almost home."

She swallowed the lump of agony in her throat. "I'm cheered," she said. It was near as they got to talking about it.

Bertha met them in the hall, as always. She was dressed to go out. Claudia had forgotten it was her niece's birthday. "The baby is nicely asleep," said Bertha. "I will be back before his ten o'clock bottle."

"I should hope so," said David. "This is the second time in three months that you've been out."

"Give a person a finger and they'll take a hand," said Claudia.

Bertha laughed. "You had a nice day, no?"

"Fine," said David. He walked on to the bedroom.

"Did you have supper?" Bertha asked, suddenly doubtful and reluctant to leave. "If you didn't, I can fix some before I go."

"We ate," Claudia lied. "You'd better hurry, or you'll miss your party."

"It is no party," said Bertha. "Just the family."

Claudia turned away from her, and followed David. This was no time to fling herself against Bertha's broad bosom for help and reassurance. This was the one time in her life that she would have to stand alone, facing her fear. It was harder than the war. In the war there had been hundreds, thousands, millions, sharing the agony of uncertainty and grief, but this was different. She and David were isolated in this special catastrophe that had befallen them.

They waited until they heard the door close behind Bertha. Then David said, "Go ahead. I suppose you won't rest until you call your precious Dr. Mack."

She knew how David felt about Dr. Mack. His letting her call him was a tacit acknowledgement of surrender. Her hand was so unsteady as she dialed the number that she had to begin over again. " What are you shaking about ? " David taunted her.

" I'm not shaking," she denied. " I was wondering, though, whether you wouldn't want Dr. Rowland instead."

He arranged his coat carefully across a hanger, and put it in the closet. " I'm not that kind of a lady," he remarked. " Dr. Rowland would tell you to call someone else anyway."

" No, he does other things, too. He takes care of Hartley's gall bladder."

" Either one you want. I'm doing this for you, not for me. I can wait until morning to find out what it's all about and why."

Claudia wet her dry lips. " There's no point in waiting." She dialed Dr. Rowland's number.

Dr. Rowland would not be back in town until the following morning, but Dr. Mack was at home, attending to business. Claudia told him what had happened. He said, " I'll be over at once. See that your husband goes straight to bed and remains absolutely quiet until I get there."

" Be prepared," she warned David, placing the receiver back on the hook, " for Dr. Mack to be his most charming and alarming self."

Dr. Mack surprised them both, however. He was extremely gentle and kind. He asked David a few questions and then took his temperature and told them, without waiting to be asked, that it was almost normal. " Very encouraging," he said, " most encouraging." He warmed the stethoscope against the palm of his hand—which was more than he'd ever done for Bobby even with a hundred and four—and listened to David's chest. " Now just one little cough, please. Don't strain yourself. Thank you—again, please—say one-two-three —one-two-three. Again—one-two-three—very good." He buttoned David's pyjama coat for him, and told him to lie back and rest. He folded the stethoscope and put it in his bag. " Fortunately," he said, " Dr. Anthony Morrisson has just returned from his vacation. I'll make an appointment for you to see him the first thing tomorrow. He's the best man in his field."

" Yes," said David. " I've heard of him." He reached for a cigarette and lit it, depositing the match, with great deliberation, on the ash tray by the bed. He cleared his throat.

" It's not too smart for Claudia to sleep in here until we know where we're at, is it, Doctor ? "

Dr. Mack cleared his throat too. " I never advise double beds under any circumstances," he said, " and I should say in this case that it would be wise for Mrs. Naughton to use another room entirely until we get the complete story."

" How long will that be ? " David asked.

" Dr. Morrisson should have a full report for us within a day or so." He rose and placed his hand for a moment on David's shoulder. " It's a nasty shock when it hits this way, but it's a blessing in disguise. What happened this evening might save you many additional months of recuperation."

" That's great," said David, with a short laugh. " That's great."

The phrase made Claudia think of white sails, and sun-flecked water, and the sharp, clear smell of clams and salt. How far away the summer seemed, as if it were a dream that had never happened. Or perhaps this was the dream, and she would wake up to find herself in David's arms. " I've got to pretend that it's a dream and that it will soon be over." It was the one way to keep on being quiet and controlled, as if she were standing outside of what was going on. David did not know that there was a trick to the way she was behaving. He said, after Dr. Mack had left, " I was afraid you'd go to pieces. It was the only thing that worried me."

" I won't go to pieces," she said. " Why should I ? Dr. Mack said everything looked very encouraging."

" Let's not fool ourselves." He closed his eyes. " Put the light out, darling, and go to bed and get some rest."

She wanted more than anything else in the world to stay with him, but it was too great a favour to ask. She rested her cheek against his for an instant, and then, without another word, put out the light and left him. The time would come when he would want her close, but now the only way she could help him was by leaving him alone. It was as if her love stretched its arms, and reached new heights.

She was afraid to undress, for it might happen again during the night. She knew it, without Dr. Mack's having to tell her so. She walked into Bobby's room, and numbly sank to the edge of the narrow cot. The room was beginning to come to life again, for his trunk must have been delivered the day before, and Bertha had started to unpack it. Piles of rumpled shorts and shirts and handkerchiefs covered the bureau, and the blue sweater was there, too, worn to a frazzle, with a ragged hole in the elbow. A great episode in all their lives had come to an end. On Tuesday, Bobby and Matthew would say good-bye to camp and the family would be together once more. For how long, she dared not think. She remembered how she had promised them that she and David would be waiting at the station, holding their small universe intact. The tears came at last and unlocked her heart with pity.

FOURTEEN

NEITHER OF THEM put the light up all night. There wasn't a sound from either room, and there was nonchalance in their greeting to each other in the morning. " Sleep all right ? " Claudia asked.

" Yes," said David. " Did you ? "

" Yes," she said. " Why don't you have a tray in bed until you hear from Dr. Mack ? There's nothing to get up for as long as you're not going to the office."

" Because I feel perfectly well, and I don't want a lot of fuss."

" Bertha won't fuss, I'll tell her that you had another attack of malaria. Dr. Mack said he'd be making the appointment with Dr. Morrisson early this morning, anyway."

" I hope he is. I've got an important client this afternoon."

She knew that he wouldn't be able to go to the office, but she didn't say so. " I bet it's my rival again," she accused him in a valiant try at levity.

" Now that you remind me, she's coming in town for a session tomorrow."

" What for ? Her house is finished."

" Nothing is ever finished with Nancy. She didn't say what she wanted but it's probably a conservatory. That's one of the few things she hasn't gone in for yet."

" She isn't flower-minded," said Claudia. " It'll be raising mink or pheasants or something of that sort."

She blessed Nancy, who, in her assorted idiosyncrasies, offered a screen, however transparent, to their innermost souls. She caught a glimpse of David's face in the mirror, as she opened a drawer of the commode to find a handkerchief. Because he did not know that she was looking at him, pain and confusion stood naked in his eyes. " I'll see about breakfast," she said, without turning back to him. " I'll eat mine in here with you."

" No, don't," he said quickly. " And keep my dishes separate——"

No wonder there was that look in his eyes. All sorts of things must be going through his mind, and chiefly that he was a source of danger to his family. " I think you're exaggerating your importance," she managed to retort.

At nine o'clock to the minute, Dr. Mack telephoned that he had arranged an appointment with Dr. Morrisson at half-past ten. "I'll call you from a drugstore as soon as I can," David said on his way to shave.

She was already more than half-dressed. "You know I'm going with you," she answered quietly.

He knew it, but he chose to argue about it because it seemed to make him feel better. He stopped only when Bertha came to the door with the baby in her arms. "No time to play with him now," said Claudia, bending over to straighten the seam in her stocking. "We have to hurry."

"Come, we see Mamma and Daddy later," Bertha told the baby gently.

"Bertha's no fool," David remarked. "She knows something's up."

"Won't you feel silly," said Claudia, "if Dr. Morrisson tells you that there's nothing wrong with you except too much smoking."

"I'll settle for feeling silly," said David.

It was but a short drive to Dr. Morrisson's office. "This is a funny old place, it looks as if he lives here, too," Claudia commented, as the taxi pulled up before an ancient brownstone house. The street had been widened sometime during the past decade or so and, in the process, the stoop had been pushed back until it was little more than an upright ladder leading to Dr. Morrisson's bronze inscription on the door. Yet in some strange way the old-fashioned house was like a landmark of distinction and indifference against the hectic encroachment of the city. "Dr. Rowlands's office is only around the corner," she went on, chiefly to make conversation, "but there's such a difference in the two places."

"Dr. Morrisson's been at this game too long to have to put on swank," said David.

"How long would you think?" she asked, while they waited for the door to open.

"Longer than I'm alive," said David.

There was no one ahead of them. The narrow front parlour was dim and cool behind the heavy, outmoded lace that covered the windows. David took a chair, and reached for a copy of *Puck*. Claudia picked up another magazine and carried it to the haircloth sofa. A moment later they were both absorbed—except that there wasn't enough light in the room to see what they were reading.

They didn't have to keep up the pretence very long, for

Dr. Morrisson was ready for them. He was a large man with white hair, and so tall that he seemed to stoop as he came to the door of the waiting-room to welcome them. He shook hands as if they were old friends. " Come in my office, Mr. Naughton, come in," he said.

Claudia started to follow, but David put his hand out to stop her. His hand was cold, even colder than her own. An instant later, the door of the office had closed upon them.

Claudia stood in the middle of the room, more alone than she had ever been in her life. There was no lonelier feeling in the world than to be outside of a closed door, waiting for news of someone that you loved. It had been different that time with her mother. There had been no waiting—no uncertainty—just the stark fact that her mother was going to die. At first it had seemed that she, Claudia, must die, too, of a grief and bewilderment beyond anything she had ever known or believed possible, but gradually confusion had blended into acceptance, and with the passing of time, life once more became complete.

The various illnesses of the children had been different, too, for David had been with her. " David had been with her." *Yea, though I walk through the valley of the shadow of death, I will fear no evil ; for thou art with me ; thy rod and thy staff they comfort me.* But that was God, not David. Only it was almost the same, because she had made David into God. Something was deeply wrong within her that she should feel this way about her husband. It wasn't love, or if it were, it was the kind of love that Bobby and Matthew felt, because she and David made life secure and whole for them. It was an ungrown-up love, becoming to a child, but not to a man nor a woman. All at once, this realization came to her. It came to her about David, too. David was guilty of the same kind of dependence to a lesser degree. When she'd almost died having Michael, a little of David had died, too. There was such a thing as being too close.

Fifteen minutes. Twenty minutes. Half an hour. What was happening behind those closed doors ? Perhaps Dr. Morrisson was telling David, at this very moment, to go home and forget about the whole thing, the trouble had come from some harmless little blood-vessel in the throat . . . but if it had been the throat, Dr. Mack would surely have known, for he specialized in nose and throat . . . yet Dr. Mack was an alarmist, and he hadn't intentionally frightened them last night, it was as if he hadn't wanted to frighten them, which was even worse. . . . Oh God, she must stop thinking in a circle. it wasn't getting her anywhere.

She walked to the window and pushed the curtain aside, and watched the traffic roll across town from Fifth Avenue. She might have been standing there for minutes or for hours, for time ceased to matter. Then suddenly, the sound of a knob turning in the door, caused her heart to twist in her breast with such violence that she could scarcely hold to consciousness. Dr. Morrisson came toward her. He was like a father, the way he put his arm around her. "Come in my office," he said. "While your husband is dressing, we'll have a little talk."

She followed him, possessed of no will of her own. He motioned her to a seat beside his comfortable, cluttered desk. She had thought she had tasted grief when, a few short weeks ago, she had sat across the desk from Dr. Rowland. She knew now, that what she had gone through then, was but a preparation for this moment.

Dr. Morrisson was kind and gentle, but he left her no room for futile hoping. He told her what he had to tell her, his fingers tented before him, his eyes a steady challenge to the assumption that she could face the truth. "The X-ray readings," he concluded, "and the determination of the various tests, which I should have before me tomorrow morning, will enable me to give you a clearer picture of his condition. Now if there are any questions——— ? "

She tried to speak. Words were hard to form. He gave her time, and then his voice was like a friendly hand held out to help her. "Will he get well—is that what you want to ask me ? "

She nodded mutely.

His eyes smiled at her. "I consider myself a reasonably well man," he said. "I keep up with the demands of my profession, and I do a day's work. Is that answer enough ? "

She stared at him, incredulous, and with a great new wave of hope washing over her. "You mean you had it too ? "

"Long before you were born."

She could scarcely take it in, he seemed so strong and vital. He was suddenly like a god to her, someone to worship and look up to. Then, all at once, it wasn't enough of an answer. Her thoughts flew to Jerry Seymour, and doubt followed swiftly upon hope. "I know someone who had it a long time ago, too," she faltered. "And this winter he got sick again, and had to go away."

"Many factors contribute to a patient's recovery," Dr. Morrisson pointed out judicially.

"His wife died. That might have had something to do with it—couldn't it ? " she implored him.

"It could."

"She seemed in perfect health," Claudia went on gropingly, "and suddenly she died. And he's alive——"

Dr. Morrisson's eyes crinkled into a laugh. "I think you're trying to tell me that, in any event, there's a strong chance your husband might outlive you."

"I'm such a coward," she whispered, in admission.

"I don't think you are," he said gravely. "I've discovered in my considerable years of practice, that what I was apt to mistake for courage was merely an appalling lack of significance."

The telephone on his desk rang. He reached for it. While he spoke, she gathered the small degree of fortitude he had bestowed upon her. She must keep her mind from flying off in tangents. There were many things that she must learn before David finished dressing ; many questions she could not bring herself to ask in David's presence.

Although it was Monday, there was a sense of holiday in the air as they emerged to the street. Not holiday, but Sabbath, rather, as if the busy world about them was muted, and everyday activity had ceased to exist for them. They stood, irresolute, on the pavement. "Perhaps we'd better go straight home," Claudia suggested almost timidly. "Dr. Morrisson said you should rest as much as possible."

"He also said," David tersely replied, "that I should wind up my affairs. Which I can't do by staying in bed."

"I know, but do you think you ought to go to the office today ? We can phone John. He'll have to know anyway."

"Naturally he'll have to know. A fine partnership I handed him." He glanced at his watch. "I don't have to meet my client until two, I might as well look in on Hartley as long as we're in the neighbourhood, and get that over with."

It was odd, she reflected, how the bond of being brothers always asserted itself in time of trouble, bridging their separate ways of life and the great difference in their ages.

"He mightn't be in," David went on, "but the walk won't hurt us."

It was far wiser to take a taxi, but she didn't say so. He

needed to keep moving, she could see that. They started to walk along the sunny street as if nothing had happened, as if they might be going to lunch at the awning café on the corner, but in reality it was as if they were lost in a dense wood without being able to see ahead. She stumbled blindly over a deep crack in the pavement. He caught her arm. "Watch where you're going ! " he commanded harshly. "One cripple in the family is enough."

Anger tore through her, restoring and tonic. "You're saying one damn fool thing after another ! " she came back at him furiously. "You ought to have your tail kicked ! "

He grinned. After a moment, he said, "Look. Thanks for not telling me how much worse it could be, and how lucky I am."

They did not talk again until they reached the wide marble steps of Julia's and Hartley's house. There was a scaffold swinging from the roof, the stone façade was getting its face washed. Hartley was as particular about the house as if it were the child that he had never had ; he was always doing things for it. Sometimes Claudia felt that it was the one real bond that existed between Julia and himself.

The butler opened the door for them. "Mr. Naughton is just leaving for an engagement," he said.

"Tell him his brother is here," said David.

Hartley joined them in the library a few minutes later. He was surprised and pleased to see them. "Well, well," he said. "Glad you caught me before I left. My sinus is kicking up, so I thought I'd get a steam at the club—best thing in the world for it—but I can put it off, no hurry about it. Sit down, make yourselves comfortable. Julia's still up in Bar Harbour, won't be back until after Labour Day. Have a cigar ? "

"No thanks," said David.

"Highball ? Martini ? I'm on the wagon myself, but it won't take a minute to mix one."

"No thanks," said David.

Hartley stood beaming at them, rubbing his hands, trying to penetrate their inscrutable faces. "Well, well," he repeated, "this is certainly a nice surprise. Didn't expect you dropping in like this in the middle of the day. I have a notion that there's something afoot."

"That's right," said David.

"There's only one thing I can think of," Hartley continued with a broad smile, "the Iceland deal's gone through at last. Congratulations."

Claudia evaded David's eyes. " Guess again," he said with a short laugh.

" Look here, you didn't come here to tell me that the deal is off ? "

" It's off as far as I'm concerned," said David.

Hartley's face fell. He'd been proud of David's getting that commission. " You were in line for it, what happened, who told you it was off ? " he demanded in rising indignation.

" Dr. John Anthony Morrisson told me," said David. " Ever hear of him ? "

" The lung man ? Sure." Hartley chuckled. " He's about the only specialist in town I haven't been to."

David gave another short laugh. " Don't let that worry you," he said. " I've done the honours for the family. We've just come from there."

Hartley wasn't very quick to catch on to things as a rule, but that deep inner tie between them seemed to serve as a short cut to his brain. He dropped into the nearest chair, as if suddenly his knees had given way beneath him. " I don't believe it," he said in a dazed way. " I don't believe it." He took out his large white handkerchief, with its fine intricate monogram, and carefully mopped his forehead. " People really do that," thought Claudia. It was like expressions you never got the sense of, until you saw for yourself what they meant. " Water off a duck's back." " Big frog in a little pond." " Grass is always greener on the other side of the fence." How often they used to have to chase the cows off the alfalfa field, or the sheep off the lawn. " If only we hadn't sold our farm——" she had appealed to Dr. Morrisson. She hadn't had to finish the sentence. " A farm is not the solution at present. Your husband has to learn the discipline of a regimented routine."

" *Sanatorium*—— " The word was on Hartley's lips, too. Claudia brought her thoughts back within the four walls of the handsomely panelled room. " The old bugaboo of sanatoriums doesn't exist any more," Hartley was saying. " They're more like hotels. I know a chap—vice-president of Sherman Motors, as a matter of fact—went out to a place in New Mexico. His wife was here for dinner after she'd been up to visit him, and she described the setup to us. It didn't sound much different than a country club."

" Those places cost like country clubs, too," David remarked.

Claudia had an impression that Hartley had wanted this

point to come up. "Forget that end of it," he begged. "Money is the one thing I've got plenty of, and you don't have to wait until I pop off to use it."

It was good for David's soul to be able to say that from the sale of the farm and a few investments, he had enough put by to see him through. "Besides," he mentioned dryly, "it looks as though I'll do any popping that's to be done before you do."

"Listen to him ! " Claudia taunted above the anguish of the thought. "Dr. Morrisson told us that people who have a little something the matter with them learn to take care of themselves and live forever ! "

"On half-rations," David added. "Many thanks." He looked strained and drawn, with that strange whiteness showing up beneath his sunburn. "Come along, Hartley wants to get into that steam bath."

"I'm not taking a steam," said Hartley. There was a stricken quality about him, as if David were his son. "This sort of thing happens every day to a lot of people," he said heavily, "but I never thought it would happen to you and Claudia. No, sir. Not to you and Claudia."

"We didn't think so either," said Claudia. "It turns out, though, that we're no different from anyone else."

They left him standing on his marble steps, a small, diminished figure beneath the swinging scaffold. "Poor devil," David said, as they walked to the corner to hail a taxi.

It occurred to her to wonder why he should feel this pity for Hartley, who had a reasonable degree of ageing health, and not a single sorrow in his life. "I feel sorry for Julia, too," she said. David wouldn't go that far. "Julia's a fool," he said. A taxi drew up to the kerb, and he helped her into it. "I wonder," he continued with his old snort, "how she's going to explain away those messages from that fake medium she swears by. I think even Hartley began to put stock in it, he seemed so sure that the Iceland deal had come to a head."

Disillusionment and bitterness sat upon him. He had called the messages nonsense ; yet, because he remembered, he, too, must have secretly wanted to believe. People did want to believe, thought Claudia, whether they admitted it or not— even strong-minded people. However, it was best not to pursue it. She let him go on calling Julia a fool, because it seemed to make him feel better, just like the way he had made an issue about her going to the doctor with him.

When the taxi turned into Beekman Place he said, "I'll drop you off——"

She had thought he was going home with her. She covered her dismay. " Are you sure it wouldn't be more sensible to let the office slide today ? "

" I'm sure," he said in a tone that brooked no argument.

" And you wouldn't want me to go with you ? "

" I wouldn't want you to go with me," he affirmed. His lips brushed the tip of her ear, and she was acutely conscious that he avoided kissing her. " Just don't worry, will you please ? I might be late getting back. There's a raft of stuff to go over with John."

" Don't skip lunch," she allowed herself to say.

" I won't," he promised.

She let him go, thinking of all the times she had nagged him to take care of himself when her anxiety had had no foundation except a suffocating sense that all was not right with him. " I've been feeling fine until this bloody thing hit me yesterday," he'd even told Dr. Morrisson. " No pun intended," he tossed in with a grimace.

Dr. Morrisson had smiled faintly. " Still, don't exaggerate its importance, very often those things are a blessing in disguise."

A blessing in disguise. Surely this was one of the truisms that could never be true. For as long as she lived, she would never get over being afraid that it would happen again. Even now, as she watched the taxi move off down the block, fear pressed in upon her. David knew that she was afraid, no matter how hard she tried to hide it. It was shameful that she should fail him thus.

FIFTEEN

" IT CERTAINLY IS a beautiful day, Mrs. Naughton."

She started violently. The doorman was newly tipped, and genial. Claudia's lips answered his smile.

The elevator man said it was a beautiful day, too. It was a long ride up to the twentieth floor, so he filled in the rest of the time by mentioning that the nurse had gone out with the baby. " Thank you," said Claudia.

The dog barked as he heard the key in the latch. He was lonesome for company, and leaped up to greet her with his great paws. " Down, Bluster ! " she cried quickly. He must be broken of the habit, he must learn not to leap up against David that way. " No strain or exercise of any kind," Dr. Morrisson had specified. Bluster was both strain and exercise. So were the children, especially coming home from camp. They'd be eager to box and fence, and show off what they'd learned. It was going to be cruel discipline for David to turn away from them. " It'll be a good thing to get off by myself," he had anticipated Dr. Morrisson, and Dr. Morrisson had agreed that in many instances it was the wisest course to follow. It might be wise, thought Claudia, but at the same time there was something needless and wasteful about it. People who loved each other ought to be together. The war was different. She had let him go almost with a sense of exaltation, because he had wanted so much to go. There was fulfilment in offering one's self to service. There was no fulfilment in being banished to months of utter inactivity.

She knew no parallel of suffering. Except Jerry. All the little things about Jerry, which she had always thought were faintly ignominious, hit her sharply in a new and stinging impact. The war, chiefly. " I'm over age," he'd merely told her. And then his constant writing in the little brown cottage up the road at Eastbrook, and the way he hadn't ever wanted to change a tire, or rollick with the children. . . . She hadn't brought up Jerry's name to David, it was better not to. They'd talked a little about Dr. Morrisson having been ill when he was young, but David was stronger than she was, he didn't have to go outside himself for comfort, or for courage.

The harsh buzz of the service bell made her realize that

she was still standing in the lounge, with Bluster regarding her expectantly. He followed her to the kitchen. Shakespeare was on the window sill, moulded into an orange-coloured square, impenetrable and remote. He watched her through closed eyes as she opened the door. An express man deposited a large and bulging pasteboard box upon the pantry floor. " Sign here," he said. " They should of ought to of tied it better, it almost came open on me."

" I'm sorry," Claudia excused the disreputable bundle. " It's some of my children's stuff from camp. It wouldn't squeeze in the trunk, I suppose, so they sent it separately."

He had a nice, sudden smile. " That's what I figured," he said. " I got a kid in camp too," he said. " A little girl."

" That's nice," said Claudia. She thought, as she lugged the box into Bobby's room, " I'm glad it's my fault that we can't have a daughter. It's one less thing for David to bear."

Anything was better than doing nothing. She opened the box, and took out the contents—some rumpled sheets and blankets, a knot of ragged socks, and a shirt with a name tape that said " Robinson." A tired tennis ball rolled out from somewhere, and suddenly Shakespeare was on the spot, coquetting it into a corner with a dainty paw. Bluster regarded the performance in disdain. Then he barked and rushed out to the lounge, and a moment later the front door opened. It was Bertha. Without wasting any time about it, she headed the perambulator toward the nursery. Her voice, full of praise and pleasure, filled the quiet hall. " Ach, what a good boy to wait so nicely—what a good, smart boy ! " Such little things made Bertha's life complete these days and gave her happiness. It was going to be hard to tell her about David.

The baby was settled in his crib and Bertha was busy unloading the carriage as Claudia entered. Lumpy bags of vegetables and fruits, selected from pushcarts with Bertha's shameless thrift, and hidden even more shamelessly from the haughty eyes of Beekman Place, emerged as if by magic. She gave a guilty little cry. " I did not know you were home ! " she exclaimed. " That notty dog did not tell me," she added, with a flash of the humour she had borrowed through the years. Claudia made a poor smile. " I haven't been home long," she said.

" I will fix you some lunch as soon as I feed the baby."

" I'm not hungry."

Bertha knew definitely then, that something was wrong, but she didn't say so. She merely swooped the baby from his crib and held him out to Claudia, his head cupped against one knowing palm, his bottom cradled in the other. " You did not see him this morning before you left," she chided gently.

" We left in a hurry."

She made no move to take the baby. Bertha was a little puzzled. " He is so sweet," she coaxed, and pointed to the silk wisps that she had combed up into a little tunnel along the middle of his pink scalp. " Just see how nice his hair is beginning to curl."

Claudia cleared her throat. " I think we slipped up on curly hair this time."

" For boys it is not important. He gained another six ounces this week. That is more important than curly hair."

" Yes," said Claudia unsteadily, " he's got to be strong and healthy. He is, isn't he, Bertha ? We'd know if he weren't, wouldn't we ? "

Bertha was slightly outraged. " Why shouldn't he be well and healthy ? He has fine parents who are well and strong."

The irony of it was more than Claudia could bear. She turned away. Bertha's voice followed her in reproach. " Why don't you hold him, Mrs. Naughton. He was just reaching out his hands asking to come to you."

It was gross exaggeration, one of Bertha's harmless fantasies. Claudia took the baby from her arms, and all at once it was as if she were holding the small image of David against her breast, and the fullness of her pity and her sorrow overwhelmed her. " You are crying ! " Bertha exclaimed in distress. " Let me put the baby back in his crib, and then you tell Bertha what is wrong."

" No, let me keep him," said Claudia, for suddenly she had the strange sense that she was holding neither child nor husband, but all of humanity in her protection. It was a kind of marriage in which, silently, she accepted the vows of an eternal union with life, for better or for worse, in sickness and in health. Love had created the burden within her arms, and it was more blessed to be rich with pain than poor with emptiness. The tears that were wet upon her lips washed away all bitterness and rebellion. She heard herself quietly telling Bertha what had happened in a voice which scarcely seemed her own.

Bertha's round face turned pale. " I can't believe it," she whispered. " I cannot believe that such a thing could happen to Mr. David."

It was strange that Bertha should use almost the same expression as Hartley. She sat down in a chair just as he had done, too numb with shock to speak. " I'll fix the baby's lunch," said Claudia.

A short while later, Bertha joined her in the kitchen. Her eyes were red. " A little piece of butter goes in his spinach," she said.

" Since when does he get butter ? "

" It doesn't hurt him," Bertha said defiantly. " I give it to him all the time." Her breath caught in her throat. " You must excuse me the way I acted. It brings back so much—when Fritz got sick, when Lisa died——" She regarded Claudia with respect. " You are much braver than I was," she said.

The strident peal of the telephone broke into the air, and gave the lie to Bertha's praise, for Claudia's knees went weak beneath her, and her heart pounded up into her throat. Suppose it was John, telephoning from the office to say that it had happened again ? She lived an eternity until she reached the instrument in the hall.

" This is Alicia Martin, Mrs. Naughton. Did you get the little note I sent to you last week ? "

Alicia Martin sounded like a friend of Julia's, but it turned out that she was a Fine Hand Laundry newly moved into the neighbourhood. " We specialize in silks and laces, Mrs. Naughton, and I can promise you that if you'll give us a chance, your problems will be over."

" Thank you," said Claudia. She sat, for a long while, in the dark hall, and Bertha fed the baby, and let her alone.

Early in the afternoon, Candy came. " John telephoned me at Greenwich," she said.

" You shouldn't have taken that long trip in," Claudia told her.

" It's only an hour. I wanted to."

They sat in the living-room, not saying very much. " I can't get yesterday out of my head ! " Candy burst out suddenly. " I don't see how you stood that dreadful trip home, not saying a word to us about what had happened, just sitting there counting the minutes till you got to shore. Weren't you afraid that——" Candy stopped, reluctant to admit the thought, or clothe it in words.

" Yes, I was," said Claudia.

" It was even worse for you than for David. Do you remember how we were talking about people worrying about each other ? Oh, damn those anchors ! You must have had a premonition."

" I've had it for a long time," said Claudia, " but there wasn't anything I could do about it. Dr. Morrisson said to be glad about the anchors."

" I'll tell John that. He kept saying, when he phoned me, that he blamed himself for not getting the new ones before we started off."

" He mustn't. That's silly."

" He was upset. He was really blaming the whole world, I guess, for letting anything like this happen to people like you and David."

" It happens to a lot of people," said Claudia, " why should we be different ? "

" I think the same thing is the matter with Jerry," Candy offered hesitantly.

" Yes."

" He's always been fine, though," Candy went on with more assurance, " until the little flare-up this winter. Anyway, he was much worse than David to begin with."

Claudia caught her up with desperate eagerness. " How do you know that ? "

" Mother told me all about it. You see, I acted so beastly about their getting married, she wanted to rouse some understanding and sympathy in me. It didn't do any good though, because I didn't have much patience with people who were sick. It just made Jerry seem more of a sissy in my stupid eyes. But now, what's happened to David has sort of made everything Mother wanted me to feel toward Jerry suddenly take effect. It's odd, isn't it ? "

" No, it isn't odd," said Claudia slowly. " I guess all that growing up means is having things happen to you, so that you can know what other people go through."

" I've never thought of it that way," said Candy. " If you boil it down, it's as good a definition as any."

They fell silent again. " Have you heard from Jerry recently ? " Claudia finally brought herself to ask. " I mean, do you know how he's getting along ? "

" Oh yes, I got a card from him last week," said Candy brightly. " He's fine, he said. Simply fine. He said he never felt more fit."

" He's not coming back here to live, though, is he ? "

" I don't think so." Candy looked frightened. " That won't
ver happen to David, will it ? I mean that he can't live
here he's going to be happy, and work ? "

Claudia shook her head. " Dr. Morrisson told me that
limate doesn't play a very important part any more."

" Then why does David have to go away at all ? " Candy
roke in swiftly.

" In the beginning, it's better. Until he learns how to take
are of himself. The only bad part of it is being afraid to
ome back, not wanting to."

" Jerry hasn't got anything to come back to," said Candy.

" I know."

" Besides, he loves Mexico. He can build a life there as
vell as here."

" You can build a life anywhere you have to," said Claudia,
hinking of Bertha. " Did John say how David was when he
elephoned you ? "

" John said he was simply wonderful, so calm, and quiet,
you wouldn't think anything was wrong. They were tying up
oose ends. There's not much to do, John says. David can
get away as soon as he wants to. They'd gotten things pretty
much in shape, anyway, on account of David's possibly going
to Iceland."

" Yes, that's true," said Claudia.

" In a way, it's almost lucky, John's being ready to take
over. I don't mean lucky exactly," Candy apologized.

" Yes, it's lucky," said Claudia quietly.

" It seems such a crazy word to use now. I thought it might
make you resentful."

" It doesn't. I wouldn't dare tell David the way I feel, but
we really are lucky in a lot of ways."

" I wonder if I could look at it that way," said Candy
humbly. " All I know is, that I feel a little guilty because this
all gives John and me a chance to make ourselves important
to you. I mean John's heartbroken, that goes without saying,
but he's so happy to be able to carry on and keep the office
going until David gets back. And then he also thought," she
went on quickly, " that you mightn't mind our coming here
to live while David's away. It might be nice to have a man
around the house, and I could be a little company to you on
and off."

Claudia was touched. " That's a fine way for you to spend
your first year of marriage. With me, and three children."

"It's a lot better than spending it with my mother-in-law," said Candy frankly.

It was almost something to smile at. "We can talk it ove later," said Claudia. "There's so much to decide, it'll take little time." She leaned her head back against the couch an closed her eyes. It was a temptation to accept Candy's offe —it might make David feel easier too—only it wasn't righ She had to get used to standing on her own two feet, an David had to get used to letting her do it.

"Are you all right ? " Candy's voice seemed to come fron a long distance. Claudia opened her eyes, and found Cand watching her apprehensively. "I thought maybe you felt fain or something, your head was back, and you were so quiet."

"No, I was just thinking."

"So was I," said Candy. "I was thinking how things hav worked out between the four of us. I was practically a bab when you and David came into Mother's life, and there wasn' any John—and now look at us. Partners and friends an everything else nearly."

"Yes," said Claudia. Her mind went back over the year: too, marvelling at the way the pieces fell into place—like ar intricate mosaic. She couldn't follow the design of it, sh would not try to follow it. It was enough to know that it was there. She was suddenly very tired. It was a strange feeling as if part of her were being wafted away. "I never get sleepy in the middle of the day," she murmured. "I don't think ever took a nap in my life, except when my appendix burst——" Her lids drooped. She was aware that Candy tiptoed from the room, and came back with a light blanket. "I'm not asleep," she wanted to tell her, "go on talking, I'm listening——"

The room was dim when she opened her eyes. David was bending over her. "Bertha said you've been dead to the world for over an hour," he said.

"I had such a wonderful dream," she whispered.

"What was it, darling ? "

"I think it was about Mamma."

He sat down beside her, and she put her arms around him, and they were very close.

She wondered afterwards whether the inspiration came while she had been asleep on the sofa that afternoon, or whether it took shape when she met the children at the station the next morning. Whichever way it was, the thought must have been within her all the time—a little the way that everything

appened in a person's life built up toward the next thing. That's
he way it had been with Bertha. First she had lost her child,
nd then her husband, yet at the very end of the road, she
ould stand bereft and stripped, but still triumphant. It made
ne realize that war, grief, separation, even death were woven
nto the very fabric of life. There had always been suffering
n the world, there always would be. You couldn't escape it
nless you wanted to escape love and living.

All these thoughts went through her mind as she stood
utside the train gates, waiting for the first passengers to
curry up the ramp. They came at last, and among them,
nbelievably tall and brown, she saw Matthew. The summer
ad changed him. The bony structure of his face was break-
ng through the childish plumpness—he was going to have a
quite large nose. Never mind, the baby would supply the
beauty in the family until Matthew had settled down into what
he was ultimately going to look like. Perhaps she had changed
to him, too, for in the moment of greeting he was shy and
diffident as if they were strangers. "Hello," he said, drawing
his upper lip down in acute self-consciousness.

"Hello," she said. "No kiss?"

Suddenly he flung his arms around her and deposited a wet
smack upon her lips. He might have grown, but he was the
same old Matthew. "Where's Daddy?" he asked.

"Where's Bobby?"

"He's coming, he was in the car behind me. Where's
Daddy?" he repeated.

She put off the moment of answering. "There's Bobby
now!" she cried.

He was saying good-bye to a group of boys as she came
through the gate. There was a councillor, too. They shook
hands. "So long, Pete." "So long, Bosto." Bosto. "They
call Bobby Bosto," Matthew explained. "They call me
Monk."

Bobby did not see them at once. He brushed past them, his
eyes clouded with the pervading sadness of leave-taking. His
first summer at camp was over, never to happen again.
Matthew didn't take it so hard. Matthew would never take
things as hard as Bobby. He kissed often and easily, and he
would be happy in his life. "Hey, Bosto!" he called out
importantly.

Bobby turned and saw them. "Mother!" It was such a
loud cry, so unexpected even to himself that people turned,
and as they saw him run toward her, they smiled in sympathy.

She held out her arms to him, but at her touch his body turned stiff and tense against her. She knew how all of his love went back into him, and churned up in his heart, and made him quiet with the pain of it. She released him "Hello," she said gently and did not try to kiss him.

He cleared his throat. "Where's Dad ? " he asked, looking around.

"He isn't here," Matthew announced. "Where is he anyway, Mother ? "

It was Claudia's turn to clear her throat. "Oh that's a long story," she said lightly. "Wait, we'll go find a cab, and I'll tell you about it riding uptown. Where's your luggage ? "

"We haven't got any, it's all sent home already," said Matthew. "Only our toothbrushes," he added virtuously, and exhibited a small, dankish package that he carried in his hand. Claudia eyed it. "Look," she said, "let's throw this away and start afresh." A refuse can stood near by. She tossed the package into it. "Where's yours, Bobby ? "

"I packed mine."

She kept herding them along before her. "What have you been washing your teeth with if your brush is in the trunk ? " Anything to make talk.

"My finger."

"I can imagine."

"He never washes his teeth hardly," Matthew volunteered.

"I do so, you sap ! "

"Shhh," said Claudia.

"Why didn't Dad come ? " Bobby reverted with a frown.

"I said I'd tell you later. In the cab."

Bobby dragged to a halt. "He didn't go to Iceland without us, did he ? " he demanded in sudden doubt.

"No, foolish. Although," she managed with a difficult nonchalance, "he might have to go away for a while."

"But not without us," Bobby qualified firmly. "Where to, Iceland ? "

"No. Not to Iceland."

"Iceland's not very cold," Matthew inserted indignantly. "My councillor said so."

"Do you want your money back ? " Claudia queried.

"What money ? " Matthew asked.

Bobby giggled. "Sap," he said. "Mother, Dad wrote you can sail a boat, and fish," he digressed with a hint of disbelief. "Can you ? "

Claudia nodded. She couldn't talk, suddenly, as she

remembered David's letters to them as full of bragging as their own. "We'll never get a cab," she said. "Just look at this crowd."

"Why can't we go straight down to the office and see Dad ? " Bobby suggested.

"Dad isn't at the office."

An empty taxi came along, but somebody else got to it first. Claudia thought, "I can't put it off much longer." She drew back from the hot glare of the mid-day sun. "Let's wait under this awning."

"Why can't we take a bus ? " Matthew demanded.

"I suppose we could," said Claudia.

They started to walk toward Fifth Avenue. It was unreal to have met them without David. She wondered if they remembered her promise: "We'll be standing here in this same spot when you come back." She had meant to hold their world intact. She was holding it for them, but not for long. They didn't know, yet, that the bottom had dropped out of it. An empty cab passed by. She hailed it. "That was luck," said Bobby. "I'd rather ride in a cab than a bus."

"I wouldn't," said Matthew. "Why can't we go down to Daddy's office ? "

"Mother told you he wasn't at the office, sap," said Bobby.

She hadn't known until this instant that she was going to do it. She gave the driver Dr. Morrisson's address.

"That's not his office," said Bobby quickly. "Where are we going, Mother ? "

"To pick Daddy up. We'll all drive home together."

"Is he building a new house at this address ? " Matthew asked.

"In a way, he is," thought Claudia. "Listen, children, I have something to tell you," she said aloud. "Dad's at the doctor's now. He had some X-ray pictures taken yesterday and some tests, and he had to go back to hear about them. That's why he didn't meet you."

Bobby squared around to look at her. "Dad isn't sick is he ? He's never sick." A note of fear crept into his voice. "What's the matter with him, Mother ? "

"A boy in camp's father died this summer," Matthew remarked.

"Shut up," said Bobby harshly. "That's a dumb thing to say."

"Dad isn't going to die," said Claudia clearly. "But he's got to go away for a little while and rest."

6

" Where to ? " they asked in a single breath.

" Oh, some place in the mountains."

Even Matthew looked a little bewildered and lost. " Are you going with him ? "

" No. I'll stay here with you children."

" That's good," said Matthew.

" It isn't good," said Bobby. " I don't want Dad to go away without us."

" Neither do I," said Claudia.

" Why can't we all go? " Matthew queried comfortably.

" Yes, why can't we, Mother ? " Bobby took up with alacrity.

" Because we have to go to school," Matthew answered smugly.

Bobby glowered at him. This was caprice of a high order. " You asked the question, you sap, so why didn't you answer it right away if you knew the answer ! "

" Don't argue, children," said Claudia. She stared out of the window. Fifty-eighth Street. They were almost there. " Children. One more thing. Dad hurt his shoulder on the boat last Sunday. Lifting the anchor. That's why he's being X-rayed. So you have to be careful not to rough-house. He's not supposed to move it very much."

" Is his shoulder broken ? " Matthew asked in awe. " A boy in camp's shoulder got broken falling off a horse."

" That was his collar-bone," Bobby corrected. " But he had to be quiet, too, and not move much."

" It's going to be a disappointment to Dad not to be able to do things with you, so don't say anything about it."

" I know. Dad doesn't like to be sick," said Bobby, with great under-statement.

He was so much like David. Claudia put her hand out, and laid it on his brown knee, so full of knuckly bone and scratches. His knees had seen hard service in the past eight weeks. " We'll have to put you in long pants, soon," she said.

" Me too," said Matthew.

" You have to grow up first," said Claudia. " And the first thing you have to learn," she added carefully, " is to shake hands like Bobby. Kissing is for babies."

" He kisses wet, too," Bobby commented in disgust.

There was nothing else that she had to tell them, and they had been told a lot, without knowing it. The thing was, not to dwell too long upon a single point. " Nobody asked how

Bertha and the baby were," she reminded them. "They're fine, thank you."

Bobby grinned. "How's Bluster and Shakespeare ?"

"Fine." Little by little, she was rebuilding their world, so that they would never know that it had crashed.

"A cat in camp had kittens," Matthew mentioned thoughtfully, "and it wasn't even as old as Shakespeare."

"Don't be a sap," said Bobby. They discussed the matter at length, while Claudia paid the taxi driver. Her knees were beginning to feel liquid beneath her, and the wild beating of her heart choked off her breath so that she could hardly greet the nurse who opened the door for them. The nurse recognized her from the day before. She smiled at the boys. "They have an appointment to be X-rayed tomorrow, not today, Mrs. Naughton."

"I know," said Claudia. "We're calling for Mr. Naughton. Is he still here ?"

"I don't believe he's left yet. Step into the waiting-room, please."

Claudia longed to break through the nurse's professional reticence. "You know all about my husband's tests and X-rays," she longed to implore her. "Tell me, tell me, don't make me wait to find out !"

"We had a nurse in camp," Matthew observed.

The waiting-room was empty again. Dr. Morrisson seemed to have no regular office hours, he apparently made his appointments with a special time set aside for each individual and weighty problem. "Why do we have to come here tomorrow ?" Bobby whispered.

"You don't have to whisper," said Claudia.

"Why ?" he insisted.

"It's always good to have X-ray pictures taken," she said.

"Are you going to be X-rayed, too ?"

"Yes. It isn't really necessary though. It's just a precaution."

"What's a precaution ?"

"Something to make Dad feel better. Darling, read a magazine, like Matthew."

"He's not reading. He can't."

"I can so," said Matthew.

This was a strange homecoming for them. Bobby's voice came to her, full of anxiety. "What's the matter, Mother ?"

"Nothing. Why ?"

"Your eyes were closed."

"Excuse me. I didn't know there was a law against it."

He laughed. She straightened his tie. He moved restlessly beneath her touch. "How much longer do we have to wait? I want to see Dad."

"I want to see Dad, too," Matthew took up. "Does he know we're here?"

"Of course not," said Bobby. "Didn't you hear Mother say we were going to surprise him?"

It was indeed a great surprise to David. He came out of the office with Dr. Morrisson behind him. He looked tense and caught off guard, but the moment he saw them his face relaxed into a slow grin, so very like the way that Bobby and Matthew grinned anyone could see that they were father and sons. Claudia's eyes met Dr. Morrisson's. "While they're saying hello," she said tremulously, "may I talk to you for a few minutes in your office?"

It was all so much like yesterday, even the words she spoke, and the way she went into the office, and the way they stood on the pavement afterwards. Only everything was so different, now. Her heart was almost singing. "This is the most ridiculous thing I ever heard of!" David protested, trying to look angry and not succeeding very well. "I feel like a henpeck, traipsing off with the whole family on my tail!"

"Too bad about you," said Claudia. "I could kick myself that I didn't think of it right away."

"I haven't said 'yes,'" he reminded her. "It's too impractical. Where do you think we'll all live?"

"Dr. Morrisson said we wouldn't have any trouble finding a house outside the village."

"I'm hungry," said Bobby, suddenly, catching sight of people eating on the sidewalk under the canopy down the block. "Why can't we eat out, and have lobster?"

"Because Bertha's got lunch ready at home."

"Telephone her to keep it for supper," said David unexpectedly. "Why shouldn't we eat out? Come along."

The menus were very large, with everything in French, and written, instead of printed. "We'll all have lobster," said David, and ordered a bottle of wine with an air of celebration.

"This really is crazy," thought Claudia. "Do you think you can wash up alone, boys?" she asked aloud.

"Gee whiz," said Bobby, in muted outrage. "Come on, Matthew."

" I don't have to," said Matthew.

" Don't be a sap," said Bobby.

" You'll notice," Claudia remarked, as they trotted off, " that they've switched from ' dope ' to ' sap.' "

" I noticed," said David. " They look great," he added, simply. " I don't think there's anything to worry about. They're all right."

" It never entered my head that they weren't. This lunch will cost a fortune."

" It should." He reached for her hand. " Darling, it isn't every day a man finds out he has a very light case of T.B."

There. He had said the words, and a great, dark mountain seemed to vanish into thin air, leaving space and sunshine in its place. " Oh, David," Claudia whispered, " everything considered, we're so lucky."

How strange that yesterday she would not have dared to tell him that.

SIXTEEN

IT MIGHT HAVE BEEN any happy day in their lives, full of the sweet excitement of the children's homecoming. Bertha was waiting for them at the door. If it hadn't been that they were on the twentieth floor, Claudia was sure she would have been hanging out of the window, watching for their taxi to drive up to the apartment entrance.

"We're going away!" Matthew greeted her with a whoop.

"But you have just come back, how can you go away?" Bertha protested. She caught hold of him on the run. "Not so fast, let me look how you have grown!"

He didn't want to be looked at. He was in too much of a hurry to savour the familiar strangeness of home, to find old possessions which had become new with absence. "I have to see if my radio still goes," he said, squirming away from her.

Claudia could sense this extreme moment of childhood. It was a shame to spoil it for him. Even Bobby seemed to have forgotten the cloud of apprehension which had hung over them on the station platform. How careful she had had to be to break the news of David's illness, to lighten the shock of approaching separation into something that they could understand and accept. Now there wasn't going to be any separation, and suddenly the dreadful uncertainty of the future was beginning to assume the colour of a challenging adventure.

"Dr. Morrison says we can ski up in the mountains all winter, he says maybe there's snow up there already!" Bobby announced with relish. He broke off to make a swift dive for Shakespeare, who emerged from his usual nowhere, elaborately aloof, but filled with purring. "Why isn't Bluster around?" he demanded. "Here, Bluster! We're home, Bluster!"

"I locked him up so he shouldn't bark and wake the baby," Bertha explained.

"You can let him out," said David. "It's all right."

"Of course," Claudia quickly agreed. "It's time the baby woke up anyway."

"A couple of good liars," said David. He knew perfectly well that there was a conspiracy to keep a hundred and ten pounds of Great Dane exuberance out of his immediate proximity. Claudia couldn't bear his knowing it. " We have to be smarter," she thought.

She was smart when John and Candy came a few minutes later. John carried a roll of blueprints under his arm, and a brief case filled with letters to sign. She wanted to say, " David's supposed to lie down and rest," but she didn't. It was time enough for that when he was away from the temptation to work. " The sooner we pull out, the better," she decided. Aloud, she said, " Why don't you and John go in the library and shut the door, the place is bedlam. Shall I tell Matthew to turn his radio off ? "

" No, let him play it," said David.

She was almost sure that there was gratitude in the look he gave her.

" I just think you and David are simply wonderful," Candy breathed. " I suppose you're doing it for the boys."

" Partly," Claudia granted, with the secret like a song in her heart.

It wasn't as easy to fool Bertha. She couldn't contain herself another instant. " What did they mean about going away, Mrs. Naughton ? Were they just joking ? "

" No, they weren't joking," Claudia said.

She had to smile at Bertha's face, exploding with mingled hope and disbelief. " You mean that we all go, too ? With Mr. David ? "

" I mean just that. You'd better start packing right away ! "

Like the children, she was aware that her voice lifted exultantly. The difference was, however, that they didn't know why they were happy, they weren't old enough to realize with their minds that one of the important things in the world was for a family to stay together.

Candy had not lived quite long enough to realize it either. " I think it's marvellous," she said, a little doubtfully, " but what about their school, and are you sure you'll find a house straight off that's big enough for all of you to live in ? "

" There's more than one kind of schooling," said Claudia, " and I don't care what kind of a house it is, it can be a shack——"

" Just so long as I have a stove to cook on," Bertha chimed in joyously.

" I'm going to miss you," Candy caught her lower lip between her teeth to keep it from trembling. " It was bad enough to have David go—but now all of you—at one fell swoop."

"You were going to lose us at one fell swoop anyway," said Claudia. "Just think, we thought we'd be getting ready to go to Iceland sometime this month."

"That would have been different. Iceland was business," said Candy.

"This is business. The biggest business of our lives."

Candy gulped. "I just think you're wonderful," she insisted helplessly. "I couldn't be."

"Everyone could be who has to be," Bertha asserted. "Come, I hear the baby awake, you can give him his bottle." She was back to treating Candy as if she were twelve years old. Poor Candy, thought Claudia suddenly, so much of living lay ahead of her before she could know the meaning and the fullness of marriage. There was something heartbreaking about youth. Impulsively, she put her arms around Candy, and kissed her.

"You never kiss," said Candy, a little awed. "It was almost as if you felt sorry for me, instead of me feeling sorry for you."

"Let's make a bargain, nobody feel sorry for anybody," said Claudia brusquely. "Come on, we'll go in and see the baby, or Bertha'll be insulted."

The baby's cheeks were like crimson velvet, but Bertha wasn't man enough to admit that it was because he was teething and not because he was gorgeous. "He is the most beautiful of the whole three," she stated brazenly.

"He has his homely days too," Claudia stuck up for Matthew and Bobby.

"He is never homely !" Bertha refuted indignantly. "Ach, don't be so ausgelassen !" she scolded Bluster, whose slashing tail suddenly hit her a smart blow across the leg. She was a little "ausgelassen" herself, what with the children being home, and the contagious sense of adventure that was beginning to take hold of the whole household. "When I fix the baby's bottle I will make you all some cocoa," she decided largely.

"Oh boy," said Bobby.

"You just had lunch," Claudia reminded him.

"I'm hungry anyway."

Matthew had ears in his stomach. He appeared on the threshold as if by magic. "I'm hungry too."

"So am I," Candy sheepishly admitted. "I haven't been

able to look at food for the last couple of days. It's the funniest thing, though, I feel a lot better about everything all at once."

" I am also a different person," said Bertha happily.

They were all having cocoa around the kitchen table, in spite of Bertha wanting to put it on a tray, when the bell rang Bluster barked loudly, and Matthew, overflowing with hospitality and a pleasant sense of things happening, raced to the door and shouted, " Yippee ! I bet it's company ! "

It was Nancy Riddle, out of a blue sky. " For God's sake," she said without preamble. She had always been afraid of Bluster, and she didn't care for cats, and she had never had, nor apparently wanted, any children. She made the living-room by the skin of her teeth, her fashionably dowdy hat awry upon her elderly pink hair. An interesting-looking box, flat and square, and weighing at least three pounds, slipped from beneath her arm and fell to the floor with a solid bang. Un-doubtedly, Nancy sensed something in the air, for she never came forth with presents for any lesser occasion than a birth or a death. This time, Claudia was certain, by the shape and the heft of the box, that she had foregone her usual contribution of a basket of fruit and had settled on stuffed prunes instead.

Bobby, who had trailed in after them, picked up the package with avid indifference. " Here's your box, Mrs. Riddle," he said, trying not to look interested.

" Run along and see what's in it," Nancy invited.

Bobby scampered off, so sure that it was candy that Claudia laughed.

" I must say," Nancy remarked as soon as he was out of earshot, " that you all seem to be very gay under the circum-stances." She stalked to the door and closed it with an air of having bought her right to privacy. " I gather," she continued, " that you haven't told the children yet."

" Told them what ? " Claudia evaded, although the reason for Nancy's visit was obvious at this point. Already she was squaring herself into a chair with the firm intention of staying until she found out what she wanted to find out. " Claudia, my girl," she announced flatly, " either you're very dumb or very bright "

" I've been accused of that before," said Claudia.

" I think," said Nancy dryly, " that I've known you long enough to guess the answer, so let's stop beating about the bush."

" I don't know any bush," said Claudia.

" Oh come now, no more of this," Nancy burst out in the forthright boom she had cultivated with the dairy business. " I know something's up, because I stopped in at the office this morning to see David, and John told me he wouldn't be in today. In fact," Nancy amended with a terse laugh, " it appeared, after a bit of conversation, that David wouldn't be in for the next several months."

" That's true," said Claudia. " He's going away for a little rest."

Nancy's eyes narrowed shrewdly. " A man doesn't drop his profession and go away for a little rest without a damn good reason. What is it, lungs ? "

Claudia could feel the hot colour flare up into her cheeks. Nancy was, and always would be, an emotional barbarian. "David's been working very hard, and hasn't had any vacation to speak of all summer." She tried to keep her voice level, but it was hard to do so in the face of Nancy's probing inquisition.

" I must say, it's a hell of a time for him to pick for a vacation," Nancy retorted with a trace of humour, " when I've just decided to get out of Angus and go into pigs. I'm going into them scientifically," she explained, " so it'll mean some real building, with cement runs and bathing facilities. Not just a couple of sheds thrown up. It's got to be a part of a planned unit."

" You've certainly got the farming bug," said Claudia, a little desperately. Yet what was she attempting to hide ? It would be simpler, and a great deal more natural to admit that David was ill, but she could not bring the words to her lips. " John's going to take care of everything while David's gone," she said instead, " so your pigs will be in good hands."

" Actually," Nancy conceded, " I like John very much. By the way, how are he and Candy hitting it off now ? "

" Fine," said Claudia, relieved that Nancy had gotten off the subject of David. " They always have."

Nancy shrugged. " More luck than brains. Oh they're in love all right, but John's a jackass if he doesn't get wise to himself and let his wife have a home of her own."

" They haven't been able to find a little place."

" Rats," said Nancy. " He's just got a blind spot when it comes to his mother—I knew her in the war. She's a great little organizer. However, it's none of my business. How long have you known about David ? "

" About David ? "

" Being run down, or needing a vacation or whatever other name you want to give it," said Nancy dryly.

Claudia kept her temper with difficulty. " David's been having malaria on and off ever since he came back from overseas."

Nancy leaned forward in her chair, and patted Claudia's cheek. " Listen, baby," she said with sudden gentleness, " don't try to fool an old lunger. I had the damn thing myself twelve years ago. What am I talking about, it's nearer fifteen. Close your mouth, honey, half the people you know have had it, or somebody in their family's had it. Or having it. It's a peculiar thing, though, how a person hates to own up to it. It used to be a standing joke with new patients at the San— they were all taking the Cure for their eyes. How much involvement has David got ? "

Claudia shook her head numbly. Nancy's admission left her speechless.

" Involvement," Nancy elucidated. " How far has it gone —one lung or both ? "

" One," Claudia faltered. " Just at the top."

" That's good," said Nancy. " My old doctor used to say, ' If you've got to get it at all, get it in the apex.' "

Claudia's tongue felt swollen against the roof of her mouth. " Was yours there ? "

" Me ? God, no. I was peppered up all over before I found out what was wrong wth me. I've got nothing to complain of, though. I'm lucky I didn't spring a cavity. How'd David find out ? "

" We were coming home from a weekend on the boat with Candy and John last Sunday. David was hoisting one of those heavy anchors——"

" And he shot a ruby," Nancy finished briefly. She smiled at Claudia's blank expression. " You'll get used to the lingo. I might be a little dated, though, maybe they've got some new way of saying it. I never had one, thank heaven, but I knew plenty who did and, believe me, it's a pretty rotten way to discover it."

Claudia nodded. Nancy's curiosity no longer seemed an affront, it was more like a warm hand held out in sympathy and affection. " It was a nightmare," she whispered. " I'll never forget it."

" No, I guess you won't," Nancy agreed, " but you'll get used to remembering, which is almost as good. Is he running a temperature ? "

" Dr. Morrisson took it this morning, and it was normal."

" That doesn't mean a blessed thing, don't let him fool you. It's the four o'clock temp that counts. Mine used to go up around ninety-nine-two, it wasn't much but it was one damn nuisance, let me tell you. It kept me flat on my back for six months." Nancy peered at the small diamond watch on her plump wrist, and heaved to her feet. " Good God, I have to get a move on, I've an appointment to get my hair done at three-thirty. Why don't I let these few old wisps grow out white, will you tell me that ? One of these days, so help me, I will." She put her arm around Claudia, and suddenly the gruffness was gone from her voice. " I'm awful sorry about this. It's not easy for a man like David to face inactivity."

Claudia swallowed. She tried to speak, but it was safer not to.

" And it's just as hard on you," Nancy went on. " Maybe a little harder. I haven't watched you all these years without getting a pretty good idea of what makes you tick. You might look as if you didn't have enough sense to come in out of the rain, but it's my guess that you're a pretty wise woman, and I've taken my hat off to you more than once—without your knowing it, of course. I don't mean the war either, you weren't the only one who had to carry on alone. It's been a lot of other things—not losing your head over that little squirt of success you had last spring, for one. How would you feel now, if you were up to your neck in a stage career ? Fat lot of comfort it would be. A career never kept any woman warm, nights."

Claudia stared at Nancy, astonished at the depth of penetration beneath her frowsy pink hair.

" This way, you've at least got nothing to blame yourself for," Nancy went on. " As a mater of fact, you've been eating your heart out about David for months. I could tell. Just by the way you asked me a couple of times how I thought he looked. I thought he looked like hell, and I told you so. But he's such a stubborn devil, what could you do about it ? "

" Not a thing," Claudia acknowledged huskily.

Nancy sighed. " Well, it's a tough road, take it from one who knows. Even when the going's good, it's tough. You can smile all you want, but underneath, you're just damn scared of living out loud, so to speak. Listen to me blow off, will you ? " She turned abruptly, and opened the living-room door. " Somebody keep that brute of a dog from knocking me over ! "

Bertha hurried to Nancy's rescue, and grabbed Bluster by the collar. " Are you going without seeing my baby ? " she asked reproachfully.

" I'll see him next time," Nancy promised hastily. " The truth is, I never know what to say to a small baby. They make me tongue-tied. Give me a horse or a cow, and I'm on my own ground."

Bertha looked as if she wanted to say that her baby was neither a horse nor a cow, but she restrained herself. " He is a wonderful, wonderful child," she got in as a parting shot.

" I'm sure of it, if he's anything like his mother," Nancy agreed.

" You are right," said Bertha, completely won over.

Claudia waited with Nancy in the outer lobby until the elevator came. " Look," said Nancy. " One more thing: remember that the doctors know a lot more than they did fifteen years ago. What with all the new theories and treatments, David'll probably be back in harness before you know it."

Claudia was more than ever touched by the unsuspected depths of Nancy's complex nature. " Thanks," she said. " I can't begin to tell you how much better you've made me feel."

" In fact," Nancy summed up cheerfully, as she stepped into the elevator, " nowhere near as many people die of it as used to."

" Oh," said Claudia faintly. She decided that a leopard never really changed its spots ; Nancy was still a bull in a china shop.

She found David hiding ignominiously in the bedroom, where Bobby was showing him a card trick he had learned at camp. " I bet you're dead," he greeted her. " John left when he heard she was here, he said she was in his hair all morning."

" Nancy had it," said Claudia simply.

It was a moment or two before David could take it in. " That old battle-axe ? " he exclaimed.

" That old battle-axe," said Claudia. " In both lungs. Go on out, children. I want to change my dress."

" I won't look," said Bobby complacently.

" March," said David, reaching for his ear like old times.

" Can't I show you another trick first ? "

" I have one too," said Matthew.

" You can't do magic, don't be a sap," Bobby withered him.

"Is ' sap ' the only word they taught you at camp, Bobby ? " Claudia inquired.

"Those were *figs!*" he came back at her in belated indignation.

She said, surprised, " Oh ?   I thought they were prunes."

" Can we come back in again in a few minutes ? " Matthew called over his shoulder.

" Yes," said David. He closed the door upon them. " Tell me more about Nancy."

She would have gladly told him that Nancy had had it in three lungs, if it would have been any comfort to him. As it was, she painted as black a picture as she dared, considering the fact that Nancy was still alive and breathing. He tried not to seem too interested, but she could see that he was following every word out of the corner of his eyes. As she talked, she made hay, and brought the thermometer from the medicine chest, much as she used to get vegetables down the children, while she was telling them a story.

" What else did Nancy have to say ? " he mumbled, with the little glass stick seesawing between his lips.

" She said that lots of people we knew had it too."

" Who ? " he demanded, as literal as Bobby.

" Oh everybody, almost," she assured him largely.

" Jerry, for one ? "

So Jerry has been in his mind, too, all this time. " Jerry is fine again," she said. " Candy got a letter from him, I forgot to tell you."

" Yes, he's as fine as he's ever going to be," said David. " I used to think he was a hypochondriac. Now I know the poor bastard couldn't help himself."

" Jerry's the sort that anything hits hard," Claudia maintained.   " Look at Nancy, would you ever have known anything was the matter with her—physically I mean—from the way she trots around ? "

" Does Nancy know about Jerry ? "

" I don't think so. If she did, she'd have said so. Nancy has no delicate reticences."

" She'd have a field day if she knew," David said. " What a lot goes on behind people's faces. I guess I'll have that kind of face from here on out."

" Oh, I don't think so," said Claudia lightly. " You look just the same as always. Keep that under your tongue, don't talk so much, or it won't register."

" It's been in long enough." He took the thermometer out

of his mouth and squinted at it. "Normal," he said, and started to shake it down.

She stopped his hand. He tried to elude her, but she was too quick for him. She knew before she looked at it that it wasn't going to be normal, but her heart sank with a sick thud when she saw that the slim thread of mercury hovered above the hundred mark. Nancy had said, "It's the four o'clock temperature that counts." Nancy had said, "My temperature stuck around ninety-nine-two for six months." This was a whole degree higher than ninety-nine-two.

"It's practically normal," David insisted.

"Practically," she agreed. This time they both knew that they were lying.

She turned away so that he could not see the shadow of fear in her eyes. She folded back the spread with unsteady hands, her fingers thick, as if they were no longer a part of her body.

"Say, stop that! I'm not going to bed!" he expostulated, in a kind of panic.

"Oh, behave. You sound like Bobby when he finds some fat on his chop."

"I'm not going to take my shirt off though," he rebelled.

"That's gratitude for you, after I let you work with John all afternoon against orders. All right, keep your shirt on, if it makes you feel more manly, but at least take your trousers off, they just came back from being pressed."

He took his trousers off, and scanned the rod in his closet belligerently. "What happened to that good pants hanger?"

"I had it on toast yesterday for lunch."

"It's mighty funny it isn't here."

"You have a persecution complex, nobody touched your pants hanger. When Candy left, did she say she'd phone tomorrow?"

"I tell you, this isn't the same one. Yes, she said she'd stop by in the morning in case you needed her."

"I do. I have to see what arrangements she wants to make about closing the apartment when we leave. I think she's hoping against hope, though, that they'll live here themselves."

"John said something about it."

"It's about time he was getting some sense in his head. Even Nancy knows what's going on."

"I told him not to go ahead with any plans," David injected, "until we'd decided definitely what we were going to do."

"What do you mean, 'decided definitely'? The way Bertha and I function, we can be out of here by the end of next week, if not earlier."

"Oh yes?"

She didn't like the look about his mouth as he said it, and yet she had half-expected that sooner or later he was going to make an issue of their going. "Now no shinanegans," she forestalled him firmly.

He lay down on the bed without answering and gave a grunt of satisfaction as his head touched the pillow. "This feels better than I thought it would," he admitted. "If I don't watch out I'll turn into a first-class loafer. Maybe I'll even take to writing, like Jerry."

"Don't be like that. Loafing's your job for the next few months."

"That may be. But it isn't your job, Claudia." His eyes were grave. "Come over here and sit down a minute, I want to talk to you."

She sat down beside him. "Don't you want us to go with you?" she asked him quietly.

"You know I do."

"Then there's nothing more to be said."

"Yes there is, and you're going to listen to me. It's utterly pointless for you to waste a whole year of your life on top of some God-forsaken mountain watching my symptoms. The theatrical season is just beginning, and you can jolly well get a move on and earn a little money for the family."

"Oh David, how noble of you!" she broke in effusively. "Do you actually mean I can live my life just as if nothing's happened, and really begin to make a career for myself? I can hardly wait. Just think of the fun, too! Night clubs. and luncheons, and parties—I've always adored that sort of thing, you know I have! But I'll keep thinking of you, darling, no matter how rushed I am, and perhaps, if I can possibly get a moment's leeway in my busy life, I'll run up to see you occasionally. Won't that be just ducky?"

"Oh shut up," he said, with a shamefaced grin. Then he pulled her down to him, holding her close but turning her head until her face escaped his lips. "Darling——" he whispered. "Oh darling——"

In all the long years of their marriage they had achieved no richer moment of love. Her heart was full to bursting.

The children were hovering outside the door waiting for her to come out. "Can we go in now?" Matthew asked.

" *May* we go in now," Bobby corrected him, gilding the lily with a broad wink at Claudia.

She shook her head. " Daddy's resting. You have to be quiet. Turn off your radio, Matthew."

Bobby searched her face, quick to take on her change of mood. " Did Dad get any sicker or something, Mother ? "

There was no use telling him about David's temperature. He was only nine, old enough to know perhaps, but not old enough to help. " No," she returned with effort, " he just has to be careful not to overdo. He has to take things very easy for a while."

" Maybe he was in the war too long," Bobby reflected, with an odd sagacity.

" A lot of men were, I'm afraid."

" Boy, when we have another war," he brooded happily, " I guess I'll be old enough to go and take Daddy's place."

" You cheer me up no end," she told him.

Bertha emerged from the storage closet with her arms full of heavy woollens. " It's good I saved everything from the farm," she rejoiced. " These are too warm for the city, but in the mountains it is freezing cold, and they will be just what we need."

" It's long underwear ! " Bobby discovered in horror.

He was so uncannily like David. Claudia moved down the hall to hide the tears she could no longer control. The kitchen offered easy refuge. Blindly, she started to take out pots and pans.

In a little while, Bertha's voice sounded behind her, full of ridiculous umbrage. " I thank you to get out of here, Mrs. Naughton ! It is too early to begin supper, and also I can manage nicely alone, thank you ! "

" You must think you're a horse," Claudia retorted over a tight throat. " It'll be a big help to everybody if you come down sick, too."

" I don't get sick," said Bertha. " You and me, we are just alike. We keep going, no matter what happens."

" I hate my health ! " Claudia burst out in anger.

" You mustn't say such a thing," said Bertha, shocked. " It is a sin for you to talk like that."

" But why couldn't it have been me ! Why does it have to be Mr. David ? "

" Because it is God's will for it to be that way, Mrs. Naughton." Bertha's voice had lost its ridiculousness. Her tones were suddenly full and stern, as if she had risen to a pulpit. "Mr. David needs you. The children need you."

Claudia's lips set in passionate rebellion. "Let it work the other way around. I need a husband. The children need a father."

"But you are meant to be the strong one."

"For what reason ! If God has a hand in all this, what is He after, what does He want to do to us ? "

"That," said Bertha, "is something I cannot answer. Often I ask myself the same question. I have lost everyone in this world—and still I go on living."

"Lucky for us," Claudia interpolated with a watery smile.

Bertha's smile was watery, too. "Maybe you and Mr. David could be some of the reason I am made strong like a horse."

"If we are, I hope you're sufficiently grateful to us," said Claudia ironically.

"Yes," said Bertha, "I am grateful. If I had to work for people I could not love it would be very hard."

Claudia wiped her eyes. "Next to Candy, I was wonderful. Next to you, I feel like two cents."

"That is foolish," said Bertha. "Nobody can be brave all the time."

Nancy and Dr. Morrisson had both told her the same thing, in different words. "No matter how light the case," Dr. Morrisson had warned her, "there will be days when you will be full of discouragement and worry," and she had answered, without fear, "I can go through anything as long as we can be together." Now fear was back upon her again, destroying all the hope and courage that had flooded her. Where had her little strength come from, and why hadn't she been able to hold on to it ? She had to hold on to it, she could not afford to be weak. Bertha was right. Four lives depended upon her, to sound the keynote of security and happiness. It was her fight, even more than David's, but at this moment she was not equal to it.

"You are tired," said Bertha. "You have a right to be tired. Lie down for a little on the couch in the living-room. I will take the children to the park for an hour before supper."

"I wish you would. It'll do them good to get away from the house. Besides, I don't want them to see me with my eyes red."

Bobby seemed to know that her eyes were red without seeing them. "It's no fun going out," she could hear him argue disconsolately in the hall. " I guess I'd better stay with Mother. Maybe Dad'll wake up soon, anyway."

" You haven't seen any of your friends for so long," Bertha cajoled. " Not since before you went to camp."

" Matthew can go," said Bobby, " but I'm too old to tag after a baby carriage and a nurse."

" Yes, you are a man already," Bertha agreed. " That is why I wish you would come along to handle the dog for me. He is so big, it needs somebody big to hold him."

There was a small silence, during which Claudia could feel Bertha's not-too-subtle flattery take effect. Ten minutes later the front door closed upon the muted bustle of their departure, and stillness hammered in her ears like noise. She couldn't bear it. She flung herself on the living-room sofa, and buried her head to muffle the sobs that ripped through her in the deepest sorrow she had ever known. Even the loss of her mother had not inflicted upon her this searing agony of confusion and uncertainty. She tried to recapture that sense of her mother's nearness which had come to her the afternoon before but the reality had faded to a memory, shadowy, and elusive. This, too, was a bereavement. There was neither past nor future. There was only the present, black with fear. She could not see above it, nor through it, nor behind it. It was a kind of death within life. The thought came to her that perhaps one had to die to be re-born.

SEVENTEEN

THE SOUND of David coughing brought her body into being again. She crept down the hall and listened with the palms of her hands wet with sweat. She did not dare to open his door, but her thoughts built into panic, even after silence once more filled his room. Would the sound of a cough always reduce her to this state of gibbering terror ! She did not need Nancy to tell her that there were those who would never get well, and no physician could promise her with any degree of honesty that David would not be one of that lost regiment of men. Dr. Morrisson had told her that his recovery depended on many things—his resistance, his environment, his natural powers of recuperation. All at once, she knew that it depended more than anything else, upon the Will of God. How often she had heard the expression without its meaning anything but words. Now it meant a great deal. It was almost as if Someone who knew what it was all about—far more than Dr. Morrisson—were standing beside her in eternal watchfulness, ready to shoulder all responsibility. It was the way a child would think, and suddenly she knew a child's obedience to this superior Presence. She went back to the living-room, and sat down, quietly, with her hands folded. Alone—amid the deep silence of an empty room—she was not alone, although David was but a remote figure at the end of a long corridor, as helpless as herself. He could not give her strength, and strangely, she felt no need of it. How odd that this should be. It was almost as if, without her realizing it, God had taken the place of David. She did not know whether it was right or wrong. She knew only that the storm within her heart was suddenly quieted, and that there was compliance in her soul. She was aware, after a time, that Shakespeare had jumped into her lap. He was asleep and purring loudly.

How long she sat there she did not know. The harsh clang of the elevator got her to her feet. She hurried quickly to open the door before the bell could ring and waken David. It was Julia.

" I thought you were in Bar Harbour," Claudia said.

" Hartley telephoned me yesterday. I took the night train, and got in this morning." Julia indulged in one of her quick, shy embraces " Chin up," she said, with a little smile.

Claudia tried to smile back, but the tears came instead. The peace and willingness that had become a part of her in the empty room abruptly vanished. Julia came from the outside world, Julia brought reality and conflict. Claudia could no longer hold her moment of vision. A black curtain of grief shut out the sunlight. She made exactly the sort of scene that Nancy had expected. " Cry it out, it wouldn't be natural if you didn't," said Julia. She opened her purse and proffered a fragment of sheer batiste, lace-edged, and perfumed delicately.

" You and Hartley have the nicest handkerchiefs," Claudia sniffed. " I hope I remember to launder it and give it back to you."

" I doubt it," said Julia. " So I might as well say good-bye to it now."

After the first conventional gesture of sympathy, there was an arresting lack of solicitude about Julia that began to have a tonic effect. " The children enjoy camp ? " she queried with her normal measure of interest.

" Yes," said Claudia.

" Is there anything I can do in the line of shopping for them ? "

" No," said Claudia. " Did Hartley tell you we were all going away together ? David phoned him a little while ago."

Julia shrugged. " That was a foregone conclusion," she said. There was no mistaking the note of complacency in her voice. " I should think," Claudia announced bluntly, getting it out of her system once and for all, " that your medium would have a pretty red face at this point."

Julia shrugged again. " I don't see why," she said.

" You don't see why ! " Claudia asked indignantly. " What about the Iceland commission he's been telling us would go through ? "

" But he didn't," said Julia, calmly.

Claudia snorted, feeling like David. Julia was not only a fool, she was completely off-balance. " How can you sit there and tell me," Claudia demanded, " that every time you had a sitting, ' V ' didn't come through with a message not to worry, it was all going to work out beautifully."

" He did," said Julia, making no sense whatsoever. " In fact, I've just come from another sitting, and ' V ' sent you exactly the same message. Why do you think I'm here ? "

" Nobody but a spirit," said Claudia grimly, " would have the nerve to brazen it out like that."

"Claudia please," Julia entreated, "stop working yourself up about 'V.' I can explain everything. It was all my fault. Actually, 'V' never mentioned one single word about Iceland. It was purely my own interpretation—and I'm sorry about it."

"Don't be ridiculous," Claudia contradicted. "Over and over again you told me that 'V' said we were going to a land of ice and snow. I remember every word of it."

"I'm glad you do," said Julia. "If you think back carefully, you'll realize that he didn't say anything about Iceland."

"I don't believe it," said Claudia flatly. "He must have. We couldn't have imagined it."

"It wasn't a case of imagination," Julia explained. "I simply read into the message what I wanted to." She opened her bag again, and withdrew a small, leather-bound book. "I have all my sittings written down. I felt the same way as you, at first, until I read them over word for word." She gave a small, tremulous laugh, as full of tenderness as a love. "Poor 'V.' We've both misjudged him." She riffled the pages, crammed to overflowing with her fine, precise handwriting. "It's all here. I'm going to have it typed out for you. Then you'll see for yourself what he's said. There's so much to read between the lines, too. I didn't realize it until I went over it all again and absorbed it anew in the light of what has happened."

Claudia could find no answer with which to blast Julia's intense sincerity. It was difficult to believe her and difficult to doubt her.

"Don't you want to hear the message that 'V' sent you today ? " Julia persisted gently.

"I suppose so," Claudia admitted.

"I'll have that one typed out, too," said Julia. "It's quite long, but in essence 'V' begs you to believe that David will be well, and that this experience will bring you a great spiritual richness and understanding." Julia put the little notebook into her bag and rose. Her hand rested for an instant on Claudia's shoulder. "Don't close your mind," she said softly. "Please try to accept with your heart, even if your brain is too proud to admit the truth of anything but clear, cold logic. We all need help, even the strongest of us, and sometimes we have to learn to take it however, and wherever, it comes. It doesn't really matter, either, for somehow I think it all flows from the same source."

"I think so too," said Claudia humbly.

A few moments after Julia left, David called out from the bedroom. " Coming ! " she called back.

He was sitting up in bed, looking rested and relaxed. " Who was here ? "

" How did you know anybody was here ? "

" I'm psychic."

She giggled, and the quick spontaneity of her laughter was as startling to herself as it was to him. He regarded her quizzically. " You seem pretty gay."

" I have every reason to be."

" That's a fine thing to say with your poor husband lying at death's door."

" I'm sorry to disappoint you, but you're not anything of the kind."

" Who said I'm not anything of the kind ? " he demanded in a huff.

It occurred to her to wonder that his spirit too, had lifted, as if a single joyous thought had wrought a miracle, and caused a wave of faith to spread throughout the very air. She knew that she must be careful not to dissipate that faith, nor in any way to challenge his contempts. Hesitantly, she told him of Julia's visit, and the message that " V " had sent to them. " You're going to be well," she impressed upon him. " That's the only thing that matters now. You're going to be well."

She expected him to taunt her for being gullible, but instead he heard her out in silence. After a moment he said, rather than asked. " You really believe it."

" I must believe it," she answered simply.

" That's different. I'll go with you on that." He reached under his pillow. " I've a present for you." He gave her the thermometer in its slim, black case. She took it out, and looked at it. The little thread of mercury just missed the normal mark.

Her heart sent up a song of happiness. It meant so little, and yet it meant so much. Dr. Morrisson had told them, with his stoop-shouldered smile. " For the next several months the thermometer will be your best friend, and your severest critic."

" This means." she translated to David as she put the stick away, " that you've got to watch yourself not to get over-tired."

" I already got the general idea," said David sourly. He caught her hand. " Listen."

" I'm listening."

"I suppose you realize that this mightn't be all beer and skittles ? "

"I realize it," she said. "But who wants beer and skittles ? I never did like skittles. What are they, anyway ? "

"This is a skittle," said David, almost kissing her.

The children tiptoed to the door. They were already in their pyjamas, reeking with cleanliness. Bertha had apparently had herself a Roman holiday, for the mark of her handiwork had scrubbed away every vestige of good looks.

"Lots of boys in camp's mothers and fathers are divorced," Matthew remarked, a trifle enviously.

"Sorry we can't oblige," said Claudia from David's shoulder.

"However," said David, "we have another very fine grade of family skeleton we can offer you."

They dissolved in helpless laughter. Matthew and Bobby joined in companionably ; they didn't know what they were laughing about, but it didn't make any difference. A cloud had lifted, and the sun was shining on their lives again.

Bertha heard the merriment, and hurried to the door with the baby in her arms. The baby was reeking with cleanliness, too, but Bertha had cheated, for instead of slicking his hair down, she had brushed it lovingly into a fluff of curls, as light as goose feathers.

"He certainly does seem to be the best-looking one of the three," Claudia acknowledged belatedly.

Bertha was not to be outdone in generosity. "The other two have their pretty days also," she admitted.

They smiled at each other. "And now I fix supper," said Bertha, who always seemed to link contentment up with food. "You and Mr. David can eat nicely on a tray in here alone, quiet, by yourselves." She seemed quite pleased with herself for having so tactfully turned a liability into an asset, but David refused to have the wool pulled over his eyes. "Nothing doing in trays, I'm coming to the table ! " he announced in a large bellow.

"Yippee ! " Matthew shouted in approval, and dashed out of the room and turned on his radio.

Bertha fled too, for David had leapt out of bed, and she saw that he had no pants on. "Do you ever stop to think," he said, as he opened his closet door, "what that woman has been to us all these years ? "

"No," said Claudia blandly, "I never do." She opened the

top drawer of the commode, and studied the contents thoughtfully. " I have too many old gloves," she decided gloomily. " Before I begin to pack I'm going to make myself give everything I don't absolutely need to Bertha's cousin."

" What cousin ? "

" Any cousin. I'm travelling light from now on, we'll probably be ending up in Iceland anyway one of these days."

" Damn right we will," said David.

" Yippee ! " said Claudia.

David started to reach for his trousers, and then got sidetracked to his dinner jacket hanging next to them. " Talking of packing," he said, " you can pack this away in moth balls, I won't be needing it for a while." He took a round box down from the shelf. " And this little silver lining can go along with it."

" That hasn't got a silver lining, it's your stovepipe hat," Bobby elucidated.

David's eyebrow climbed his forehead. " You don't say," he said. " I thought it was prunes."

" Let me pop it," Bobby begged. " I like to pop it."

He popped it, and David stuck it on his head at a rakish angle. He looked very funny in a stovepipe hat, with no pants on. Bobby let out a ribald hoot, and Matthew left his radio to come racing in to see what he was missing in the line of fun.

The radio started to play a waltz. " Madame, may I have the honour ? " David said to Claudia.

" The honour," Claudia told him softly, " is all mine."

They moved around the room, David in his stovepipe hat, and Claudia in a pair of long white gloves. It was scarcely more than a slow, sweet walk in each other's arms, but to the children it was dancing, and their laughter still kept on.